Unheard Melodies

Unheard Melodies

Warren Leamon

LONGSTREET PRESS
Atlanta, Georgia

Published by
LONGSTREET PRESS, INC.
2150 Newmarket Parkway
Suite 102
Marietta, Georgia 30067

Printed in the United States of America

1st printing, 1990

Library of Congress Catalog Card Number: 89-063789

ISBN 0-929264-26-6

Design by Laura Ellis.

For my mother
Martha Coleman Leamon
who gave, though free to refuse

PART
1
1948-49

I walked uneasy on my youth's fine lawns
And sought for definitions . . .

—Brian Higgins

Uncle Luther, back from the war, stares through the smoke that rises from his cigarette. A thin red face, circles under the eyes. His hands tremble as he raises first his drink, then his cigarette to his mouth.

There is something wrong with him. It has to do with the war, but it has to do with something else. Everyone feels sorry for him.

After he has gone, my mother, her eyes full of tears, says, "They ruined him."

"Sure they did," my father says. "Hell, he was thirty-six and had a heart murmur. They shouldn't have drafted him."

After that I don't see him, only hear about him. Uncle Walter, Luther's brother, brings news of him, his drinking, the jobs he loses. Uncle Walter, who is wealthy because he "made a killing" in the cotton business during the war, seems to be in charge of Luther, a task that weighs heavily on him. "What can I do?" he often asks my mother. "He's our brother."

The words come back at night in the dark bedroom as I lie awake. The words mingle with the steady breathing of my brother. The words — "war" and "made a killing," "our brother" and "ruined." And over and over again, "they." "They ruined him . . . They shouldn't have drafted him." An alien force. A power beyond Uncle Luther's control. Do "they" make him drink and lose jobs, too? Is it "they" who make Uncle Walter say, "What can I do?" The words revolve around the image like smoke: thin red face, circles under the eyes, hands that tremble.

Uncle Luther has come home from the war.

-1-

For a long time I would remember that year because of Minnie. Only when my own life moved beyond my control and made me begin to question my beliefs about winning and losing, about success and failure, did I begin to think of it as the year when Aunt Mary came. But Aunt Mary came every August so that year was, somehow or other, a typical year, no different, really, from all the years before and though I was standing on the old basketball court when I saw Aunt Mary coming, I know now that I might as well have been in my grandmother's room, a room that reached out and encompassed my world with all its irrationality and contradiction, a room in which Old Gene Talmadge's eyes stared down from one wall, FDR's from another.

In that room my grandmother kept a shoe box full of strange and wonderful things: Florida postcards and pressed flowers and old photographs in which the lips and flowers of the women were tinted red and a picture of a man hanging from a tree and Civil War coins and medals and mementos from the Atlanta Cotton States Exposition of 1896. New South Boosterism and lynchings merged with dashing colonels and exciting battles, the glory of which she summed up with her resounding cry, "The Yankees didn't whip us, they just overpowered us!" Although born in 1878, she remembered vividly the Burning of Atlanta. And placed carefully on top of the shoe box—as though the box were an altar—was the faded black case lined with dark blue velvet that contained a cracked flute, the very instrument played by my ancestors at Waterloo, at Seven Pines and Cold Harbor. From time to time she let me handle it and in those moments words in books, "history," became solid, something I could touch, the cold metal of the stops.

"Did Grandpa play?" I asked.

"No. He had scarlet fever when he was a boy. It left him practically deaf."

So that explained why, in a family descended from flute players, there were no musicians, no music in the house.

Is it true that she grew up on a farm in middle Georgia? It must be since official records don't lie. But official records don't tell the truth, either, and by the time I knew her she was so thoroughly a part of the city that I still can't believe the ground we buried her in was not the same ground she sprang from seventy-eight years before. Alexander Street, Georgia Avenue, Piedmont Park, Grant Park, Five Points, Westview Cemetery itself—she seemed to embody the names.

When I was very little she would walk with me to the lake that was near our house. Actually it was little more than a large pond, probably created by a builder to enhance the value of his subdivision, a part of the rampant growth that destroyed my world. But in my memory the lake is always associated with silence, a silence so complete that on a summer day I could hear a screen door slam over a block away. And in the winter the cold gray sky seemed an extension of the cold gray surface of the water, gray silence reflecting gray silence. Maybe I was holding the hand of my grandmother when I first saw it, but my most vivid memory is of myself, all alone, sitting in silence beside the lake.

Or sometimes she took me with her when she went shopping. Six feet tall with large limbs and high, pronounced cheekbones and long hair that she swirled into a bun on the top of her head—how impressive she was as

she strode up the hill to the bus stop; and how she domi-
nated the bus itself as she moved down the aisle, glaring
at those who had had the temerity to take seats near the
front. And even when seated she seemed (maybe because
of the black wide-brimmed hats she wore) to tower above
everyone else. Anyone would think that she was riding the
bus not to get anywhere but merely to see what it was
like, to see firsthand the unfortunate creatures who *had*
to ride in it. She didn't discriminate in her sense of super-
iority. Her eyes swept scornfully over black and white
alike. But the blacks, forced to sit in the back of the bus in
those days, had to bear both the disapproval of my grandmother and that of the society at large. I wish I could say
that I sympathized with their plight. A little epiphany
would be nice, an anecdote in which I'm sitting next to
my grandmother and I see a black forced to the back of
the bus and suddenly I'm filled with guilt over my unwit-
ting participation in racial oppression. I've read such
anecdotes but I've never really believed them. To the child
the world simply *is*, a fact. Eventually the fact would grow
more complex, would finally explode and dissolve into the
greater mysteries of time and space. But it was to be a
long time before I realized that it wasn't only World War II
but also another more distant war and the reconstruction
that followed it that had created the city I was born into.

In those days Atlanta began where the Peachtrees join
at Baker Street. The miles between my house in Buckhead and that intersection were neither rural nor urban
nor even suburban. The large houses on Peachtree gave
way to apartment houses—solid brick edifices with one
screened porch on top of another. We passed Brookwood
Station, where the train still stopped to pick up pas-
sengers; then at Pershing Point, West Peachtree lay
straight and hilly before us and the apartment houses

(mostly older wooden and brick ones) mingled with small office buildings. Finally the bus (or trolley) pulled the last hill, West Peachtree rejoined Peachtree and the city rose before us: squat, dowdy and pleasant — a provincial brick and mortar overgrown town.

On those shopping trips we mostly stayed in the area stretching from Baker Street to Lucky Street. Only rarely did we catch a Shoppers and go past Five Points. And when we did I felt as though I was entering a foreign land. Already my vision of the city was sharply different from that of my grandmother. For her the area around Davison's must have been a new and chic appendage to Five Points, the heart of the "real city" she had known when she first came up from the country. Probably she didn't even realize how seldom we went past Five Points to Rich's — didn't realize it because it existed so firmly in her mind, in her past, that it would always be Atlanta.

In short, my grandmother had been superceded, but just as I couldn't know that Atlanta was a provincial city, so I couldn't know that my grandmother was an anachronism. She represented for me a way of thinking, a way of seeing the world.

When my mother was playing bridge or shopping I got a good insight into my grandmother's world view, for on those long afternoons she ruled the house with her terrible moral strictures: lying would rot your tongue, ghosts of dead relatives watch us constantly, illness is a punishment for sin. Her Friday night soup was a kind of metaphor for her attitude toward life in that it might contain anything: beans, cabbage, fish heads, ground beef, carrot ends and — according to my father — socks, false teeth, eyeglasses and toothbrushes. A thick brown mixture we closed our eyes and ate just as I closed my eyes and accepted whatever reality she summoned up — ghost, ancestor, God, Satan—when she caught me lying, cheating or stealing.

But my world was full of anachronisms. A coal chute ran from the driveway to the basement. A truck came by the house several times a week to deliver blocks of ice for our box on the back porch, and, if we ran out, we could go to the ice-house in Buckhead. There were even two chickens in our backyard, right there in the middle of Buckhead.

They hadn't always been chickens. They had begun the previous spring as two of thousands of red, yellow, blue, green and orange chicks. Grotesque little creatures that were, for some reason, deemed cute, they milled about in large open-topped cages, "peeeeeping" incessantly. You plunged your hand down into the teeming mass of poultry and pulled out the squirming color of your choice. I suppose that, being newborn, they were thought of as appropriate to the Easter celebration. Certainly they made as much sense as the fat pinkeyed bunny rabbits. And they were brightly colored like the eggs. Add the gaudy sashes that held in the white dresses of the girls, and—if the moon cooperated—the dogwood blossoms that lined the streets, and you had a full-fledged pagan rite of spring, complete with great crowds of people gathered at dawn on Stone Mountain or in their cars at drive-in theaters, their eyes fixed on the rising sun.

Actually, the chicks were a far better symbol of the crucifixion since most of them, because of the coloring, died within days, or at the most weeks, after being taken home. And since all of them went to city or suburban homes, their deaths were, as my family was to find out the hard way, a mercy.

Because one spring, for reasons as mysterious as the Easter season itself, our chicks—an orange one for my

sister, a blue one for me—did not die. After a week my
mother grew a little anxious and after two weeks, when
the color was fading away, she began to watch them
closely, especially when we had to take them out of the
little cage we had built. And finally, we made the fatal
mistake of naming the creatures. Rhett and Scarlett we
called them. I think my sister made the suggestion and
my mother probably smiled ironically since, even though
they had survived for two weeks, it was inconceivable that
they would live much longer, that they could survive both
the dye and suburban life. But as spring gave way to
summer and the orange and blue colors disappeared and
the chicks grew larger and larger and messier and messier
and louder and louder, all smiles faded from her face.
Whenever she suggested getting rid of "them," we
responded with mournful pleas for the lives of "Rhett and
Scarlett." For they had become, willy-nilly, those most
revered and dreaded members of a family—pets.

Now the families that surrounded us were either
southerners like ourselves, trying to escape the stigma of
their backgrounds, or Yankees who had come South to
escape theirs, but who didn't fancy themselves as having
moved to the land of cornpone and pellagra. It wasn't
that they never saw any live chickens. Mr. Castleberry, in
overalls and smelling of the farm, came by every week in a
green pickup truck and sold us eggs and butter and
vegetables and occasionally a live chicken. But almost
immediately my grandmother disposed of the creature by
grabbing it by the head and swinging it round and round
above an open garbage can until the body broke loose
from the head and shot into the can, onto which my
grandmother slammed the lid and waited until the thrash-
ing and squawking stopped. The neighbors never even
saw the headless chicken run around the backyard for a

few moments. These chickens, however, were running around in the backyard, day after day, with their heads on, clucking and scratching and, from time to time, crowing.

So our neighbors, Yankee and Confederate, came together in their attitude toward Rhett and Scarlett. They frowned, they shook their heads, they uttered sarcastic asides, but of course they never confronted us directly, never said straight out, "Stop turning the neighborhood into a farmyard." It was a good neighborhood, really, despite what my father thought; we minded each other's business quietly and politely.

But expressways were being planned even as the chickens scurried to get out of the way of the coal truck and I watched the ice truck spraying water on the street; streetcars were being replaced by trackless trolleys that drew their power from overhead electric wires. And I had hardly grown familiar with trolleys before diesel buses took over completely. Later, when I rode with my father in the car on rainy nights and he cursed the slippery old streetcar tracks that threw us about from time to time, it never occurred to me that we were sliding over the relics of a transportation system that had twice been superceded in my own ten or twelve years. It seems that everything became an anachronism almost as soon as it came into existence.

And in August Aunt Mary came.

I was playing basketball by myself on the old asphalt court owned by the Catholic church less than a block from my house. I felt like a trespasser, but my obsession with basketball overrode my Protestant scruples and I spent hours by myself, shooting baskets and playing make-believe games in which I roared up and down the court, winning championship after championship in the last second. I was in an arena in Boston or Lexington or Los Angeles, not on an outdoor basketball court between a cathedral and a delapidated convent. I paused to let my feet cool and wipe the sweat from my eyes and she materialized out of the heat: at first a distant form no more substantial than the shimmering rays that rose from the pavement; then, as she descended the hill that fell from Peachtree Street, a shape, a figure clad in black from hat to lace-up shoes; and finally the woman herself, the ramrod straight back (even though the body was pulled to one side by the black suitcase she was carrying), the high breasts, the thick stockings, the exquisite ivory cameo of a woman's profile hanging from her neck. And when she reached out and put her free arm around me and pulled me to her, the heavy odor of lilac water.

"Mary!" My mother's voice as we walked toward the house. And then the yearly ritual.

"You should have called. We would have picked you up at the bus station."

"Oh, I don't want to be any trouble."

"It's no trouble. You shouldn't be out in this heat. And carrying that heavy suitcase."

"I don't mind. In fact, I like riding the trolley."

"Well, let the boy carry your suitcase for you."

"Oh, no. I can carry it. It's not heavy."

"Don't be ridiculous. Here, take your Aunt Mary's suitcase."

She wasn't really my aunt. She was my grandmother's niece, which made her my first cousin once removed, I suppose. (My generation was probably the first in the South to lose the knack of keeping degrees of kinship straight.) But whatever the kinship, it was close enough to give her the right to our home every summer. And once again, Aunt Mary had come for a visit.

Crossword puzzles were her passion. It was as though the empty squares represented the mystery of life and the day couldn't begin until she had filled them all in, so every morning I settled down with her on the sofa in the living room. How often did she stun me with "aloe" for "medicinal herb" and "peri" for "Persian sprite" and "ewer" for "pitcher"? When she finished, she held the paper in front of her eyes. "There. All done," she said, removing her glasses. (The stems were joined by a delicate chain, and when she wasn't reading or working puzzles, they hung down across the top of her breasts.) She was always cheerful, yet she cried more easily than anyone I have ever known; tears filled her eyes at the most trivial misfortune, though she always smiled as she cried. All in all, she was a curious mixture of nun and efficient secretary, and in fact her faithfulness to her job and to her boss, who had taken her with him when the company's headquarters were shifted from Atlanta to Charlotte, in later years took on something of the devotion and sacrifice of the religious.

"I swear, Mary, I'm getting suspicious," said my father at the dinner table. "Mr. Kelley taking you off to Charlotte that way. Are you sure it's your work he likes?"

"Oh, no. I mean, yes. Calvin, he's a married man."

"I know. But still . . ."

"You mustn't say such things." Tears filled her eyes but she kept on smiling.

"Of course he shouldn't," my grandmother said. "Calvin, you ought to be ashamed."

Mary, riveted with embarrassment and shyness, could only say, "Thank you, Kate," as she took out her hankerchief and dried her eyes.

My father's joke didn't seem cruel to me, or even

insensitive. It was simply irrelevant. The idea of Aunt Mary having an affair was preposterous.

For a person adventurous enough to come all the way from Charlotte to our house on buses by herself, she was strangely immobile once she arrived. Perhaps she viewed the journey as a struggle through a hostile world and felt safe only when she was surrounded by her cousin's family. Her black clad figure moved from bedroom to kitchen to dining room to living room and in the late afternoon to the porch at the front of the house, where the family sat after dinner when it began to cool a bit. Then Mary talked eagerly about Atlanta, about the old streets around the capitol where she had grown up, about the Tenth Street district where she had lived for awhile with her brother and sister. Georgia was "The Empire State of the South," Atlanta "the Phoenix risen from the ashes." The clichés of the city's public relations men became on her tongue sincere realities, and one who didn't know better would have thought the city she described had nothing to do with the slow moving, rather large Southern town we were sitting on the outskirts of. Growth was in the air then, change was synonymous with progress and the middle-aged woman dressed in black rocked on the porch on hot summer afternoons and described lovingly the town she had moved through as a girl as well as her vision of that town, gathered from the local newspapers, a sort of enormous version of her own past.

But however much Aunt Mary might want to fade into the house, she had to make one trip. Every year she went to Milledgeville to the state asylum to see her brother Bud, who had been committed before the war. This year, like every other, my father offered to drive her there and as usual she refused, refused even to be driven to the bus station. She rode the trolley to the station and rode the bus the fifty miles to Milledgeville. She returned that evening.

"How was Bud?" my mother asked her.

"He seemed very well. I . . . I think he may have recognized me."

And after she had gone to her room, my mother shook her head and said, supposedly to me but really she was talking to herself, "She says that every year."

"Maybe he *is* getting better," I said.

"He can't."

"Why not? I mean, it was an injury. Maybe . . ."

She smiled. "She told you the story about the fireman's net?" (Bud had been a fireman and, according to Mary, during a practice drill he missed the net and landed on his spine, which resulted in injury to his brain.) "It wasn't the accident. It began before that. It began with Dave."

"Dave?" I tried to remember who "Dave" was.

"Never mind. You're too young. I'll tell you all about it some day."

But I was to find out a little about it very soon. Or at least I was to be reminded who Dave was. One morning my mother told us, "Your Aunt Bessie is coming." Aunt Bessie was Aunt Mary's sister. "Now she'll be very upset. You're too young to understand but you mustn't make it worse for her. And you mustn't ask about your Uncle Dave." Then I remembered. Dave was Aunt Bessie's husband, the one she had run off with.

When my father heard that Aunt Bessie was coming, his countenance turned grim and then the lines deepened in my mother's face. The house was filling up with women. Young as I was, I knew what she feared. And the neighbors' silent discontent with the chickens was becoming more and more apparent and my mother stared out the back window at the creatures and asked what to do about them and my father said, "Nothing, goddam it. Yankee sons of bitches. We'll do what we want with our property." Of course, my father hated the chickens as much as anyone else, but he hated the neighborhood more than the chickens. He had grown up in rented houses in sections of the city that contained nothing but rented houses. And though for awhile he built and sold houses I don't think that he ever wanted to own one and certainly not one in a middle-class neighborhood where he suspected that people were always poking their noses into other people's business. My mother had simply confirmed his suspicions. But before he could continue his tirade, my grandmother came into the kitchen and accosted us.

"I can't find my shoe," she said.

"Shoe? What shoe? What are you talking about?"

"My dark blue velvet shoe."

Actually it wasn't velvet—they had already argued about that—but my mother accepted the definition. "Have you looked for it?"

"Of course I've looked for it. Everywhere. It's gone."

"Well, it'll turn up."

"It's gone, I tell you. It's been stolen."

"Oh, Kate, don't be silly."

Grandmother rose to her full six feet and glared at my mother.

After supper, as Mary and I worked the puzzle, my grandmother turned her irritation on us. "I don't know what you see in those puzzles." She said this practically every night, but tonight her voice had a particular edge to it.

"I enjoy doing them. Working it out."

"It's a waste of time. Pointless. Filling up a bunch of little boxes."

"You learn things," I protested. "The meanings of words."

"You don't learn anything that way. You learn from experience. Experience is the best teacher." She said it as though she had made it up.

So maybe I was trying to get even with her when, after we finished the puzzle, I got out my geography book and pretended to be studying it. "Grandma," I asked, "what's it like at the South Pole?"

"You know. I've told you."

"Tell me again."

"Hot. O Lord, it's hot. You see, the further south you go, the hotter it gets, and the South Pole is the hottest place of all. Full of jungles and monkeys."

"No, it's not. It's cold."

"Don't be silly. It's burning hot."

"It's cold. It's covered with ice."

"It's hot, I tell you."

Triumphantly I spread my geography book in front of her and pointed out a picture of a vast expanse of white ice. "There. *That's* the South Pole."

She stared at the picture.

"See." I pointed to the caption beneath the picture and read very slowly, "A picture of the South Pole."

"That's wrong."

"It can't be. It's in the book."

"They got mixed up. That's the North Pole."

"No, look." I had anticipated this and I thumbed quickly back to a picture of the North Pole.

"It's the same picture," she said. "They're both the North Pole."

"No. You see, the earth is round and . . ."

17

"The South Pole is hot," she said, standing up. And she walked out of the room.

For two days the missing shoe hovered like a flaming sword before us. We searched the house from basement to attic; we raked the front and back yards, hoping to find it beneath the leaves. Grandmother talked about nothing else. Mother became nervous, irritable. "Just like her son," she mumbled over and over. Grandmother mumbled too, mostly unfinished sentences. "Thinks I'm an old . . ." "Stolen, but they . . ." "Since she's never here, she can't . . ." "Experience is the . . ." Not even my father escaped. He was working hard trying to finish two houses before the bank foreclosed on his loan, and because he wasn't drinking, when he came in, generally after dark, he ate quickly and went to bed. He had "walked the straight and narrow" (as my mother put it) for a long time, and since we were all eager that he should continue on that path, we trembled when Grandmother brought up the shoe. At first he only grunted and ate, but we knew he could not withstand the pressure of bank, weather *and* Grandmother for very long.

And then Aunt Bessie arrived from California. Late in the afternoon, while we were sitting on the porch, she pulled up in a taxi. A handsome woman, straight-backed like her sister, but with larger, higher breasts. And colorful—flowers in her hat and prints of flowers in her dress. And boisterous. She hugged everyone, laughing all the time. To me Aunt Bessie didn't seem "upset."

I had never seen both my aunts at the same time. They moved about the house like dog and cat. Bessie jolly, outgoing, laughing and teasing; Mary shy, withdrawn, her eyes often misty above the grin that seemed etched on her mouth.

"I swear, Mary, it's unnatural. You never go out," said my grandmother.

"She's afraid she'll melt," said Aunt Bessie and laughed.

"Well, at least I went to see Bud." For the first and only time that I can remember Mary's eyes almost flashed. "Why should I go all the way down there? He doesn't even know who I am. Or who you are."

"You can't know that. Not for sure."

"Oh, don't be ridiculous."

"Well, I say it's unnatural," my grandmother insisted, as though she had just discovered something. "You ought to get out."

Unnatural. The word stuck in my mind. I asked Aunt Mary what it meant.

"Well, it means 'not natural.'"

"What's 'natural'?"

"It's . . . it's what everybody does. Or is supposed to do. It's natural for fish to live underwater, for instance."

I had just brought home a puny little bream.

"It's natural for birds to fly," she added.

"I see."

"But . . . but it's more than that. I mean, it's natural for you to love your mother and father."

"And my brother?"

She stared at me and I realized what I had said. I hadn't meant what she thought I meant. "I hate my brother," I said quickly. "Does that mean I'm unnatural?"

"You don't mean that."

"Yes, I do. I hate him."

"Well, you can't help how you feel. But you can help how you act. You still have to be his brother. You have to help him if he needs help and be loyal to him. Just like you have to obey your parents."

19

Labor Day brought the annual family reunion and at ten in the morning we all crammed into the car—my father and mother, my grandmother, my brother and sister, Aunt Bessie and Aunt Mary and myself—and drove to Piedmont Park. Several large tables had been pushed together on level ground near the lake. A few other relatives were already there, and by twelve o'clock the area swarmed with aunts and uncles, nieces and nephews, mothers and fathers, grandmothers and grandfathers and cousins ranging from first to sixth. Most of the men were either farmers up from the country in middle Georgia or city dwellers who had left the farm and now worked as painters, bricklayers, carpenters, plasterers. Large, big-boned, red-faced men who wouldn't have been out of place at an eighteenth-century English country fair. The women—short, tall, fat, thin—were quick about the table as they laid out platters of ham, chicken, eggs, potato salad, cakes, pies and great pitchers of iced tea and lemonade. The hot sun beat down on the lake, on the drifting swans and ducks, on great expanses of grass going brown, on crowds of people at other tables, on my own relatives standing, sitting, squatting, paper plates heaped with food held in large bony hands.

I played with the other children, only one or two of whom fell in the lake; careening in and out of groups of adults, I was held up occasionally by a cousin or uncle I didn't know who insisted that I must be my older brother. One, Uncle Thad, actually my great uncle, an enormous man with a belly that pushed out and over his large belt, lifted me in the air and swung me about. Another, Uncle Walter, told me about the current cotton market, apparently suffering from the end of the war. And more than one pale-faced smiling woman asked me if my grades were good. The day waned, the sun grew hotter and the swans drifted serenely on the lake, indifferent to our shouts and cries. Since I seldom played with anyone, I was inept at the children's games, but I knew that I was supposed to play with them. After awhile, however, I slipped away and sat at the foot of one of the tables.

"So you just up and left," said Uncle Thad.

"Yes. I couldn't take it anymore," said Aunt Bessie.

"Well, I'll tell you. I liked Dave, but he was a bit of a drinker."

"And if Harry thinks someone is a bit of a drinker . . ."

Everyone laughed. While trying to remain inconspicuous I shifted about so that I could see some of the faces.

"What will you do, Bessie?"

She looked determined. "I'll go back to California. Not to him. But I can get a good job there."

"And another husband?"

Laughter.

"Well, at least she saved you, Mary."

I was sitting at Mary's feet. I looked up and saw her blush, moisture rising to her eyes. "What are you talking about?" she mumbled.

"Come on. We all know about you and Dave."

"He always liked Bessie. We were just good friends. He and Bud and I. We were all good friends."

Laughter.

"When two sisters go after the same man, look out."

"The two prettiest girls in town. I'll tell you, a hard-drinking traveling man will get 'em every time."

"He didn't drink then," said Mary.

"Oh, ho, just good friends!"

Loud general laughter. The circle of faces seemed to grow redder, the eyes gleamed more brightly, but Mary kept on smiling though her eyes were filled with tears.

"See, she's still sweet on him!"

Mary lowered her eyes and saw me. "Good lord, what are *you* doing here?" She reached down, grabbed my arm and as she stood up dragged me to my feet. "Come on, young man. This is grown-up talk."

"Come back, Mary. We were only teasing."

"Come on, Mary."

But we kept going until we had climbed to the top of a small hill. I could see the park surrounding us on all sides, the lake and the swans, and in the distance the buildings of the city. Mary was looking at the skyline when she spoke to me.

"You shouldn't sneak up that way. Why weren't you playing with the other children?"

"I didn't want to play with them. I don't like them."

"Yes, you do."

"No, I don't. I don't like them."

"Well, you should play with them whether you like them or not."

"Why? You don't."

She looked at me. "What do you mean?"

"You didn't like them so you ran away. Why can't I do the same thing?"

"It's not that I don't like them. It's . . . They're wrong. That's all. I can't stand them being wrong and believing what they say."

"Wrong about what?"

"About Dave and me." She looked away again, back toward the city. "It wasn't *me* that Dave hurt. And it certainly wasn't Bessie. But I can't tell them that."

"Why not?"

When she looked at me her eyes were full of alarm, as though she had suddenly realized whom she was talking to. "I just can't, that's all. You're too young to under-stand. Someday I'll tell you all about it. Look," she said and her face brightened. "They're beginning to clean up."

I looked down at the tables and saw that she was right. I looked back at Mary. She stood between me and the sun, a black shape rimmed with a bright glow. "When we get home, we'll do the afternoon puzzle," she said.

We made our way back to the family. Mary led. She walked very carefully and watched where she was going as though we were moving through a jungle rather than over smooth hard ground, but still she stumbled every now and then.

"You really shouldn't be so sensitive," my grand-mother said when we got back to the tables. "You prac-tically ruined the day for everyone."

Mary was already helping put things away. "I'm sorry, I didn't mean anything," she said.

"Oh, you never do."

My mother watched but said nothing. Then she looked at me. "Go play with the others till we get ready to go," she said. "I mean it. Go on."

Three days later both sisters left. My father drove Bessie to the train station where she began her cross-country ride back to California. Mary returned to Char-lotte. As usual she refused to let my father drive her to the bus station, refused to let me carry her suitcase, and at eight in the morning she kissed us all and walked off. I went to the street and watched her. She became a black figure, pulled down on one side by the suitcase, as she struggled along the sidewalk and up the hill to the bus stop, where she became a distant form coming and going as the traffic flashed between us. Finally, a bus came, and when it pulled off, the bus stop was empty.

That afternoon I sat on the sofa by myself and tried to work the crossword puzzle. I was surprised at how much I could do without her there, but still I managed to fill less than half the boxes (my greatest triumph, one I bored everyone with for weeks, was "ideate" for "to think"). I could understand the clues but, like Mary when she stood between me and the sun—a shimmering rim of light around a dark center—and said, "I can't tell them that," I lacked the words.

-2-

But the chickens didn't go away. Even at the time I wondered how they lasted as long as they did. I mean, I wondered why no one took the law into his own hands and killed them or took them away. Or something. Now I realize that the neighbors were probably *afraid* of them. If you haven't been around them much, full-grown chickens are fearsome beasts. And the truth is, after Labor Day came and we started back to school and I walked home every afternoon, I *hoped* that they would be gone. At first the thought of them being wrung into the garbage can to squawk themselves to death appalled me. But gradually and without my realizing that it was happening, I came to hate those ugly creatures that were always there in the backyard. But every now and then I also hated my mother or my father or my sister or my brother or my friends, and I didn't want to see their necks wrung. Not really. Thus every time my mother mentioned "doing something" about them, I joined my sister in a mighty wail of protest.

It was, alas, a question of loyalty and betrayal. Everyone — my mother, my grandmother, the neighbors — wanted to get rid of the chickens. Everyone, that is, except my sister. But before my mother could do anything, she had to have our — mine and my sister's — permission. I think I would have given in but when I hinted at it to my sister, her eyes filled with tears and, trembling, she said, "No, not Rhett and Scarlett."

So every morning I left my grandmother's world — in which the South Pole was hot, the sun revolved around the earth, one million was the biggest number of all, ghosts stopped the eight-day clock and chickens roamed the backyard — and entered the world of the school, in which everything clicked smoothly along according to numbers and laws. Proof? I could choose the printed words on the pages of the books that were written not by individual men but by great infallible machines that simply stamped facts on pages — not unlike Aunt Mary's crossword puzzles; or I could choose the words of my grandmother, words that were true because "experience is the best teacher."

But I could not really escape my house. My classmates began to talk about "the farm" and make chicken noises as they passed me in the hall. And every morning as my brother, sister and I walked out of the house, Grandmother's voice followed us, reminding us how much her shoes had cost. And my sister and I (my brother had the good fortune of having to practice football) dragged slowly home in the afternoon to be met with Grandmother's account of how she had spent all day looking for the shoe. "It's been stolen," she said again and again. "I tell you, it's been stolen." Mother gazed sadly at us and shook her head.

"For pity's sake, Kate," my mother said. "Forget the shoe. You have to think about Minnie. She keeps asking about you."

My grandmother's eyes narrowed.

"You ought to go with me. I can't keep making up excuses. After all, she's *your* sister."

"She doesn't want to see me."

"Yes, she does. She asks for you every time."

"I'll go. Sometime." Then her voice hardened. "*After* I've found the shoe."

More than ever I slipped out to the Catholic basketball court where I spent hours by myself, shooting baskets and playing my make-believe games in the heavy afternoon

silence. But occasionally, particularly when the days short-
ened and grew colder and my hands ached and my heavy
breathing poured clouds of mist before my face, I heard a
faint tinkling coming from the convent building. And several times a tall, dark shape draped in great folds of cloth
from head to foot appeared on the hill beside the court
and motioned to me to go away.

She was a nun, and the noise — the chimes — had
something to do with their secret rituals. That was why
she motioned me away. But how did she know I wasn't a
Catholic? How could she tell that? Whatever the answer, I
obeyed her; I clutched the ball to my chest, scrambled up
the hill — not the one she was standing on but the one
that rose to East Wesley — and slipped through the hedge.
Once beyond the hedge I was beyond the church
grounds, out of her reach, beyond the domain of priest
and nun and chimes. I wasn't afraid in the sense that I
thought I would be captured or injured. But in those
moments when she towered above me, I felt that I was in
the presence of something alien, something I didn't
understand. Afterward, the feeling translated into a sense
of injustice — no one else, no Catholic, wanted to use the
court, I couldn't possibly see or hear what was going on
inside the convent, and anyway, I didn't care about their
rituals, their "communions" and "sacrifices" and "sacra-
ments." All I wanted to do was play basketball. But as my
mother pointed out, it was their property, and the sa-
credness of property was something I did understand,
even when I was only ten or eleven. They, like everyone
else, could do what they pleased with their property.

What possessed me, then, and caused me to invade
their inner sanctum, to go into the towering cathedral
itself? Curiosity, of course. I had heard that the small
building next to the cathedral that was used as the rectory

had once been a kind of general store and that a tunnel ran from it to the old convent, which had been the home of a prominent member of the Ku Klux Klan. So Klansmen would go into the store, then pass through the tunnel to the house, where they planned their evil deeds, their beatings and lynchings. And rumor had it that the basement of the cathedral intercepted the tunnel, that if you went through the wooden doors between the two sets of stone stairs that formed semicircles rising to the entrance to the cathedral, you could get into the tunnel. A preposterous story, probably the remnant of some scurrilous anti-Catholic legend that held that Catholics *were* the Ku Klux Klan and only pretended to be anti-Catholic as a cover so they could persecute non-Catholics, especially blacks and Jews. But to me it was all like something out of an adventure book: tunnels and secret meetings and violent deeds. For a long time I had plotted with a friend to sneak in, but he always backed out. Then, on a cold day when I stood on the basketball court cradling the ball in my arms, my back against the wind, my face toward the cathedral, I decided to go it alone. The wooden doors were locked and, thinking there might be another way into the basement, I climbed the steps to the great doors that led into the cathedral, pushed one of them open and stepped inside.

I found myself standing next to a stone cistern filled with water. My eyes went up, followed the massive stone columns to the high ceiling. Winter light filtered through the stained glass windows that lined both walls, barely illuminating strange elongated figures. And before me lay the long center aisle stretching to a raised area on which stood the altar. And above the altar, on the wall behind it, a larger-than-life Christ hung from the cross — so huge, so realistically carved I could make out, even in the dim light, the lines that defined the chest, the ribs pressing against the taut skin of the midsection, the calf muscles, the bulging veins in the arms. I had come in looking for adventure, looking for a secret tunnel. Now, standing in the cold air (I could see my breath dancing faintly in front of my face), surrounded by the stone walls and columns, I seemed to have entered a vast cave to discover the remnants of an old pagan cult. I felt myself being drawn down the center aisle toward the figure on the cross. I could see the nails driven through the palms of the hands, through the overlapping feet. The head, with its circle of thorns, hung straight forward into the wing-like V of the arms. I paused, stood in the middle of the rows of empty pews and tried to make out the eyes, but they were buried in dark shadows. I stood for a long time in the empty silence before I heard the hissing sound. At first I thought it was the wind, but I soon realized that it was coming from inside the building. I looked around, trying to discover its source. I remembered the nun standing above me on the hill. I was closed in, trapped. Sneaking onto a basketball court was one thing, but now I had violated the church itself, descended into the depths of its demon worship. Here no nun would motion me away. I expected the figure on the cross to come to life, to swoop down upon me. And when I looked back at the crucifix, the transformation began.

The arms changed color, turned black and flattened into wings—massive, motionless wings that absorbed the boards behind them. The crown of thorns became a tuft, high and red, as the round piercing eyes came out from the shadows and formed on either side of a long, hooked beak. The mangled overlapping feet merged, grew into enormous tail feathers stretching almost to the altar. Only the midsection with its bloody gash remained unchanged.

I closed my eyes and opened them to find the man-vulture still there only now the creature was straining to pull away from the wall, to swoop down on me.

I turned and fled up the aisle. I threw a glance back over my shoulder, but before I could see anything my body slammed against something and I fell to the cold hard floor. The hissing was louder now, almost at my ear, and I imagined the creature hovering close above me, its great wings flapping slowly as it descended. I rolled over on my back, lifted my hands to ward off the attack and saw, far down the aisle, the man hanging on his cross.

I rose slowly, pulling myself up on what had knocked me down, the stone cistern. I knew what was in it—holy water. It was a part of Catholic magic, used to ward off evil spirits. Slowly I extended my hand until my fingers touched the surface. It was cold, cold as the sweat that was drying against my body. I looked back down the aisle and shouted to the crucified man, "It's only water!" and plunged my hand down until my fingers jammed against the stone at the bottom. I pulled my hand out and stared at it, first at the palm, then at the lines of bones and veins that ran from the wrist to the knuckles. Nothing had happened. It was only water. The man on the cross was a wooden man on a cross carved out of wood. And as I was passing out of the church I noticed against the back wall a steam radiator, like the ones in my own house only larger, and I knew where the hissing noise had come from. I only imagined it all, I said to myself, and I thought that once I was outside my fear would fade. But as I walked home the neighborhood too seemed silent and menacing and the wind stung my damp hand.

On one of those threatening days when clouds gather at the edge of the blue sky and the wind rises and begins to strip the last leaves from the trees, my mother, sister

and I sat in the living room listening to the radio. Grandmother, we were told in tones colder than the rising
wind, had gone to the police station to report the theft of
her shoe.

My father came home earlier than usual, an ominous
sign. My sister and I peered out the window at him as he
moved from his car to the porch. His coat collar was
turned up against the wind and he stared down at his
feet. His hands were jammed deep in his pockets. He
entered the living room.

"What's wrong?" Mother asked.

"I've just been to the bank. They're hounding me."

"Oh, no."

"The weather forecast is for rain, maybe ice. That
means we won't be able to work for God knows how
long."

"Everything will work out."

He glared at her. "Both my bricklayers are out drunk. I
don't know when, if ever, I'll see them again. One of my
carpenters is in jail for drunk and disorderly and I have to
go downtown to bail him out."

"Be calm. Don't get upset. You know . . ."

"Goddam it, I know what you mean."

"Calvin! The children!"

"To hell with the children. I work my butt off all day,
then go and have some fat banker tell me he's going to
foreclose on me. My workers don't show up. A flood is
about to set in. And now I have to drive downtown to bail
a drunk carpenter out of jail. Why, I don't know, since he
can't work in the rain."

The door flew open and my grandmother entered the
living room. "I made my report," she announced.

My mother shook her head furiously.

"Report? What report?" my father asked.

"To the police, of course. I swear, Calvin, you never think about anybody but yourself."

He stared at her in utter bewilderment.

"I reported the theft of my shoe."

"Shoe?"

"My shoe. The one that was stolen."

At that precise moment a great gust of wind burst through the open door and seemed to knock my father upright. His whole body bulged. "Your shoe? Are you still off on your shoe?"

"Of course. You don't just—"

"Your goddam shoe. Shoe, shoe, shoe. That's all I've heard for days." He was glaring at her. He moved toward her. She backed up slightly and raised her umbrella a little.

"Somebody stole it, you say. Somebody came into the house, went through the living room and dining room and kitchen and bedroom. Then went upstairs into your bedroom, into your closet, and took one shoe and left. Is that what happened?"

Silence.

"Somebody—some *man*—passed up radios, coats, money, appliances and risked years in jail in order to steal one shoe. Is that it? Is it!" He was shouting in her face.

"There are people who will do anything."

"You're right. You're dead right about that." He looked around him, at my mother, at my sister, at me. Then he looked back at Grandmother. "You're a goddam bitch. You know that? A—"

"Calvin!" my mother shouted.

Grandmother literally rose to the occasion. Her large breasts seemed to swell under her jacket, the bun of hair rode on her head like a crown and the umbrella in her hand took on the appearance of a sword. "I know about these things. Experience is the best teacher, I always say."

But by now she was talking to the world at large because my father had walked out the door. Through the window I watched him back the car out of the driveway and roar away in a great swirl of dead leaves. An hour later he hadn't returned. He missed dinner. My mother's face grew tense.

I climbed the stairs to my bedroom. At the top my grandmother stood in the doorway to her room and beckoned to me with her finger. Since my sister slept on a cot in the room, she was already there, the covers pulled up to her chin.

"You shouldn't pay any attention to your father when he's that way," she said.

I nodded.

"He gets mad and he doesn't know what he's saying."

I nodded again. Apparently my grandmother thought my father had said something that hurt *me*, but I couldn't imagine what she had in mind. I heard my sister sobbing. Wind rattled the windows and through them I could hardly make out the black swaying shapes of trees. We heard a car door slam. Or was it a garbage can lid blown off by the wind? We strained to hear. The front door opened and closed with a loud bang.

"Margaret!" my father shouted. The name thundered through the house. "Margaret!" We heard the sound of something falling. A vase? A lamp?

"Stop shouting." My mother's voice was barely audible. "The children . . . asleep . . ."

"That damned mother-in-law of yours!"

"Shhhhhhhhhhhhhh!"

"It's not Bud who's a lunatic. It's her. Your goddam mother-in-law. *She* ought to be in Milledgeville."

Then only muffled voices and the sound of footsteps as they moved down the hall to the bedroom.

The three of us in the room upstairs said nothing. We were all lost in the same thought: how long would this bender last?

During the days that followed, my mother was frantic. She called mutual friends late into the night and tried to catch him on the job. He came home only for brief periods, red-faced and reeking of cheap blended whiskey, shouted a bit and then left. Grandmother stayed out of his way but she lectured me on the evils of drink and on demons that prey on the souls of heavy drinkers. Mother attributed it all to heredity, to what she called "a weakness that runs in the family." Putting my grandmother's and mother's views together, I could only conclude that "demons run in the family," a not very wholesome prospect for the future.

In school all mysteries of existence were explained under the general heading of "evolution," a term none of us — including the teachers — really understood beyond one generality: just as fish had become apes and apes had become men, so men would inevitably become something else — bigger, better, happier in the vast economy of the universe. And the earth revolved predictably around the sun, no matter what our eyes told us. And any mystery — such as why birds migrate or salmon climb the streams to spawn — was a mystery only because we did not yet have enough data. The future of Atlanta, the very city in which I lived, had been foretold a hundred years before when John C. Calhoun pointed to the junction of two proposed railroad lines on a map and predicted that a great city would grow there. I was now inexorably a part of that growth which was in turn a part of that other growth called evolution. The New South rang through the class-room daily, one with the multiplication tables and the stationary sun. I, with a father on a bender, a mother a nervous wreck, huge chickens roaming the backyard and a grandmother calling the police station daily about a stolen shoe, longed to believe my teachers.

And in the house itself I found a place of escape. Or rather, I built one: I partitioned off a musty dark corner of the basement with old blankets; it was always late November in that room, dark and damp and cool. In it were an old desk, a rickety chair, a smelly moth-eaten rug and a bookcase filled with an incomplete set of the Harvard Classics. The bookcase and books had come from Uncle Walter, who bought them to complete the furnishing of his den and, when he moved to another still more expensive house, gave them to us. Most of the books, when I came upon them, had never been opened, and many pages were stuck together by mildew. I think I tried reading them all at one time or another but my favorites were the *Odyssey* and the *Rubiyatt* (which I had heard was erotic, but I supplied most of the eroticism). At night, sitting under a single naked lightbulb, I read and daydreamed. Especially when my father came in roaring and singing and my mother tried to calm him and get him into bed, I blocked out the noise overhead with my fantasies: I walked alone in the fall, wind whipping my body. I was world famous, yet I was solemn and aloof. I had a past, I had fought in a war, done hard labor, almost starved. I was hardened to life, yet sensitive.

It was on one of those nights toward the end of his bender when my father was tapering off and my mother could make him at least half understand what she was saying that the strange word first came to me, its hissing sibilants slithering down the winter chill of the staircase.

A hot sound, like sex and sin, alive and fleshy and evil. It was something that Aunt Minnie had "tried" but the word that came before it had lacked its malignant force, had dissolved in the dark cold staircase. Maybe I had heard the word before but on this night, as I drifted among new incomprehensible visions, it got past my ear and twisted around the breasts and thighs of naked women. And then disappeared into darkness, into other words, into the rising voice of my father as my mother urged him down the hall.

Gradually he returned to normal although the hangover was ferocious: he vomited relentlessly, his temples pounded visibly, he sweated profusely. He ignored my mother and growled at my grandmother, more or less daring her to cross him. But he went back to work and not much damage was done. The last bender had lasted two weeks and had required a week of recuperation. Mother was relieved; she even sang a bit as she cleaned the house.

Just before the Thanksgiving holidays I trudged into the front yard. It was a dark dreary day, swept by a cold wind filled with forebodings of winter. Probably the weather caused me not to notice the . . . silence. And the house was quiet as well. My grandmother was in the kitchen cooking. My mother was in the basement washing clothes. Still, things were too quiet. Then my grandmother asked me to take out the garbage. I went down the back steps, emptied it into the can and was back in the kitchen before I realized that not only had I not heard anything, I hadn't seen anything either. I went to the kitchen window and looked out.

"Where are Rhett and Scarlett?" I asked.

"They're not there?" She came over and looked out the window. "I don't know where they are."

Neither did my mother, who professed great surprise and went out into the backyard to look for them. "I don't know," she said. "It's very strange."

My sister wept. "You've killed them," she moaned.

"No, we haven't. They'll turn up." Though how chickens could "turn up," I didn't know.

"You killed them!" she cried. "You've killed Rhett and Scarlett!"

We ate late, as usual, because my father was trying to make up lost time. And sitting in the middle of the table was a large platter of . . . something. It wasn't fried chicken, which was the only kind of chicken I had ever had since it seemed to be the only way my grandmother knew to cook it. But lying under a thick layer of sauce on a bed of rice was what certainly looked like what chicken wings and breasts and legs might look like without the crust.

"Here, I'll serve the plates," my mother said and I passed mine to her. She filled it, then my sister's, which was strange. We were always served last. And my mother seemed oddly cheerful, asking questions, joking, laughing. I poked my fork into it and watched my sister do the same.

"What is it?" my sister asked.

"Duck," my mother almost shouted. "You've never had it before. You'll love it."

My sister fished a leg up and studied it. Then she looked at me. Our eyes locked in a profound truth that neither of us would ever voice, that would remain forever a silent truth. But I didn't understand what her eyes said at first. I pulled up a wing and looked at it. I knew what was on the plate, of course, and I didn't want to say anything, but my sister was younger, wasn't as wise as I had become, and I couldn't betray her. "I don't think

this . . ." I never got any further. A great pain in my leg
stopped me and it was a moment before I realized that
she had kicked me. I looked at her. A frown was frozen on
her lips and she moved her head very slightly from side
to side.

"Go ahead and try it," my mother said quickly. "You'll
love it."

And then I watched my sister tear a bit of the flesh
from the bone with her fork and thrust it into her mouth.
"Oh, yes," she said, "it's wonderful." And as she chewed
she smiled — a smile that contained not a trace of irony. Ah
me, what layers of hypocrisy and betrayal were in that
smile. What layers of hypocrisy and betrayal had been in
those tears. And then I remembered my own cries of protest, how I had stood by her, right up to the last minute.
It was all a knot I would be years untying. Only when I
abandoned my Protestant forebears and came to understand what "ritual" meant would I understand that evening. But for now the sighs my mother and grandmother — and I'm sure the whole neighborhood — heaved
were enough. I dug in with the others and we ate Rhett
and Scarlett.

After our act of cannibalism I went down to my
"room" in the basement and sat with a churning stomach
in yellow light. I had come down to read, I even held a
book in my hands, but my eyes were locked on the concrete blocks that my father had erected against the earth
and I wondered whether all families were like mine. The
other children, my classmates, seemed normal and sane,
but I probably seemed normal and sane to them, so that
didn't prove anything about their homes. Did they have
lunatic relatives in Milledgeville? Did chickens roam their
yards until they pretended that they were ducks and ate
them? Did their grandmothers believe that the South Pole

is hot, that thieves break into houses to steal one shoe? Maybe we—myself and all my classmates—were participants in a game that we didn't know we were playing. But who did know?

A creaking on the stairs brought an end to my reverie and then, as if to confirm my fears, my grandmother, a newspaper in her hand, pushed aside the old blanket.

"I want you to go downtown with me in the morning," she said.

"What for?"

"Look." She opened the newspaper to a back page that contained police notices. One of them stated that stolen goods to be claimed would be on display. I started to argue with her. I had come over to the side of logic and science and was convinced that neither her ghosts nor her morals nor her soup could prevail against reason—no one would break into a house to steal a shoe. But I loved going downtown so I held my tongue.

My father, however, didn't. "Are you crazy?" he asked as we sat at the breakfast table, "You're going all the way downtown to look for that damn shoe?"

She met him squarely. "Yes, I am. Shoes don't just disappear."

A strange statement coming from a woman who believed in ghosts. I wanted to ask her *why* they didn't.

"All right," my father said. "All right, damn it. Let's go then."

"I prefer to go on the trolley."

"No. I wouldn't miss this for the world. We're going together. Come on." He reached out to grab her arm but she jerked it away.

"If you insist." And she strode out the door to the car.

My father practically dragged my grandmother into

the police station where an old sergeant asked us what we wanted.

"Her shoe," my father said. "She's come for her shoe."

"What?"

"You don't know about her shoe. What kind of a policeman are you?"

"Now look . . ."

"What he means, Officer, is that I have come to examine the stolen goods you have recovered."

"Oh. All right. What are you missing?"

"I don't see what that has to do with it. I just want to examine the goods."

"Look, lady, you tell me what you're looking for, then I let you in. Otherwise you could claim anything. See?"

"I wouldn't do that."

"Of course *you* wouldn't, but there's plenty who would."

"Humph! You treat law-abiding citizens the same way . . ."

"Go ahead, tell him what you've come for. Tell him."

There was a deafening silence. My father grinned, I fidgeted and the sergeant stared, expecting almost anything, I suppose. My grandmother stared, too.

"Well," said the policeman.

"A shoe."

"A what?"

"A shoe."

"You mean a pair of shoes."

"No, dammit," said my father. "She means a shoe. One shoe. You see, someone broke into our house and stole *one* shoe."

"A blue velvet shoe," my grandmother said, "of very good quality. Size nine and a half."

"And that's all?"

"That's all."

"Look, if you just want to look at the stuff, all right. We'll probably have to auction most of it anyway. But you don't . . ."

"She means it," my father said. "I swear to God she means it."

He stared at the three of us for a moment. "In there," he said.

We entered an enormous room filled with tables covered with radios, clocks, clothes, guns, knives, silver, dolls, cheap jewelry, books, bottles, lamps — an incredible jumble, the residue of a shockingly inept underworld.

It was hopeless. I was filled with both joy and pity — joy that my grandmother was brought face to face with what I had come to consider her folly (I could never bring her to this point over arguments about the South Pole); pity that she should be so brutally exposed. I looked at her, expecting the worst. What I saw was an enormous ridiculous grin. She walked through the maze of tables to one at the far end of the room, leaned over and pulled from the debris a single blue shoe. She examined it. "Size nine and a half," she said. "Mine."

My father's face went beet red, whether from embarrassment or rage I couldn't tell. She marched past him out of the room to the desk sergeant. We followed.

"Here it is," she said. "My shoe."

The sergeant looked at it. "No, ma'am, it ain't velvet."

She threw back her shoulders. "It *is* velvet."

"It ain't."

My father swallowed and said, "It's all right, Officer, the shoe wasn't really velvet."

"But she said . . ."

"It *is* velvet."

41

"Goddam it, it's not!" my father shouted. "It never was!"

"Take the shoe," the sergeant said. "Take it and get out."

"No. I insist upon signing for it — signing for a blue *velvet* shoe."

They stared at each other. "All right!" Now the sergeant was shouting. "Sign for it! Here! Sign for it!"

And she did.

-3-

Maybe it was all a ritual. I know that it's fashionable now to think of reality as a game—or rather, as countless games. But I know about games; I was raised on them. Football, basketball, baseball. And so I know that games end. Somebody wins, somebody loses and it's over. And no two games are exactly alike. But ritual possesses a terrifying sameness. Peripheral details vary but at the heart of every ritual the eyes stare out at you, stare out from a reality beyond the finish line of any game. One replays games. One relives rituals. They never end. They live on in things, in words. Not long ago, but long enough ago, before I knew that I had to go back to discover what ritual my own life was reenacting, I stood on a mountain-top with my wife and we watched a bird—a redtail hawk—turn great circles in the sky. Below us, stretching as far as the eye could see—were the colors of the autumn mountains. "It's beautiful," I said and she said, "Well, you wanted to sit at home and watch football. You just remember that I was the one who told you to come." Familiar words that drift with the hawk over the years, bring the memory of other birds, mockingbirds pecking the red berries out of magnolia pods. No, that would be late autumn, too early for ice. It was a winter day—grim, raw and overcast. I'd been playing on the outdoor basket-ball court and I'd fallen on the asphalt and skinned my knee. It ached in the cold air and I stood in the backyard rubbing it. The grass was no longer brown; it was gray, a small barren expanse beneath the huge black trunks of the oak and elm trees. I was waiting for my mother to come out of the house and unlock the car because once again I had to go with her to see Aunt Minnie.

My mother came out carrying the pillowcase filled with Aunt Minnie's laundry. She tested the back steps to make sure that they were not icy and then descended them quickly. Her body was wrapped in a thick brown coat that was at once fashionable and bulky.

Aunt Minnie lived on the far side of the city, and in those days you had to drive through the main business district to get there. The massive stone and brick buildings, stark and stern in the cold air, hung together like stodgy powerful elders staring out of eyes that reflected the cars on the streets and people on the sidewalks who seemed to move aimlessly, man and machine dazed by the season. And then we came to streets that were lined mile after mile with long low warehouses, grim and silent and broken occasionally by small cafés and shops. Through grimy windows I could make out men and women hunched over tables and counters.

The heater threw thick warm air into the car. I leaned against the door, pressed my face against the glass and watched the buildings give way to woods, bare trees strung with dead kudzu, great patches of naked black-berry bushes—gray mazes of limbs and trunks and stalks flashing by, dotted here and there by small settlements of cheap prefabs and trailers and older wooden houses with rusty torn screen porches and smoke curling up into the dim sky. Yards were littered with tin cans, old newspapers, the rusty hulks of gutted cars. Every now and then there was a dog, large but scrawny, chained to a tree or to a line running between trees. Children in coats much too large for them stood in the red clay yards and watched us pass. I had seen those children before—or rather, I had seen those same eyes staring out of family photo albums, the eyes of cousins I had never met or couldn't remember. Children in Rowena or Warm Springs.

I would have been one of those children if my father hadn't had what my mother called "get up and go."

We turned up an unpaved road. Fall rains had washed deep ruts into it, ruts now frozen into sharp ridges and mounds, and we bounced along, my head at times brushing the top of the car. Finally there came into view, bouncing up and down with my eyes, the old brown house — really more of a shack — surrounded by small twisted pine trees that rose out of hard red clay. There were two other houses beyond, both deserted, their windows shattered, their roofs caved in. And off to one side was a small lake, probably dammed and filled with water years ago by a farmer before he discovered that the land he was trying to work and the animals he was trying to raise on it needed much more than water.

The main room of the house was small, the walls covered with paper depicting large roses on a yellowing background. In one corner was a small black coal-burning stove which belched smoke at the connection with the flue so that the room was suffused with a milky haze and filled with the odor of coal and kerosene. Aunt Minnie sat in an enormous overstuffed easy chair, its large flat arms soiled and greasy and indented with circles made by bottles and cups. She was wrapped in a bright red shawl that fell over her lap. Her legs were covered halfway between knees and ankles by a black dress and the rest of the way by thick, sagging rayon stockings. Her face was large and bony, the chin falling over a thin neck, but her cheeks were so sunken they appeared as large vein-marked holes on either side of her nose. And her eyes were huge, deep and dark, nothing more than shadows though I was often told that I had her eyes, an observation that sent shivers down my spine. Now the shadows were fixed on us. Like the face of a great bird, a hawk or a vulture.

"How are you, Minnie?" my mother asked.

She nodded.

"Are you warm enough? You really should get that stove fixed. I don't know how you stand all this smoke. And why do you keep burning kerosene lamps? The electricity has been turned back on."

She pushed me toward the spindly sofa. I sat on it and she sat next to me. The vinyl was cold and I squirmed a bit.

"Where's Kate?" the old woman asked.

"She's still a bit under the weather. She can't seem to shake her cold."

"She just don't want to come."

"That's not true. When the weather gets better she'll be here all the time."

Aunt Minnie shook her head.

"Of course she will. Now tell me, how have you been? I was telling Calvin the other day . . ."

And my mother began one of the monologues that constituted these "visits." She ranged over everyday affairs, described telephone conversations in detail, whole meals were cooked, served and eaten, chance encounters on the street turned into momentous occasions. I had a built-in clock that told me almost to the second when my mother would rise and say, "Goodness, I didn't realize the time," and pull me up. That second was drawing deliciously near when Aunt Minnie leaned forward, interrupted my mother's flow and said, "You should've seen him at the end."

"I know, Minnie, I know."

"He was nothin'. Nothin'. Skin and bones. Yellow. Yellow all over."

"I know. But you mustn't dwell on it."

"The doctor killed him. He coulda got better but the doctor . . ."

"Why don't you go outside," my mother said to me. "Go on."

I didn't need to be told a third time. I made quickly for the door.

"The only one left, Margaret," Aunt Minnie whined. "And the oldest. All gone."

"You mustn't dwell on it. It's been months."

"'The Lord giveth, the Lord taketh away.' Well, all he's done is take from me. Why couldn't . . ."

The door closed behind me, shutting off the smoke, the smell, her words.

As I wandered down to the lake, I remembered how, when we had come in the summer, the dust choked me. Now the ground was frozen into rock-like ripples so that I had to be careful not to stumble. I thrust my hands deep in my coat pockets, hunched my shoulders up around my neck and watched my breath dance in front of me. The water reflected the sky and the pine trees, and the reflections shimmered in the small ripples the wind stirred every now and then. Except for the muffled sound of a car passing unseen on the road a half mile away, silence hung over the land like the low grim clouds. I picked up a flat pebble and skipped it across the lake. It bounced three times and then sank and I watched the four shattered images of trees and sky gradually reform on the surface. I tried to imagine what the place had been like sixty years before when my aunt had come here from middle Georgia, but then I remembered that she had first lived in the city. My grandmother had talked about a boarding house, about a husband who was a house painter and drank too much. Bits and pieces.

The door to the house slammed and my mother called my name. I turned and half ran toward the car, anxious to get back to my own warm house, to my own backyard. As I was opening the door my mother snapped her fingers and said, "The laundry. I forgot it. Run in and get it."

I returned to the house and entered the smoky room without knocking. Aunt Minnie sat motionless in the chair. I saw the bundle of laundry in a dingy pillowcase lying in the corner. I picked it up and turned to leave.

"You got any girlfriends?"

I was so startled, I flinched. "No, ma'am."

She leaned forward in the chair and whispered, "I was married twice, you know?"

I don't know whether I knew or not.

"Had to marry the first one. We went skinny-dippin'." She giggled but it came out as a grotesque gurgle. She raised her hands to her breasts. "These weren't flat then. No siree. I had nice big ones. Not too big. Just about right. Jack, he used to say, 'Anything over a handful is wasted.'" Her giggle became a cackle, screwing up her face and bringing her dark eyes out of their shadows. She leaned further forward until her hands, still clasping her breasts, were pressed against her knees, like an image in a dream, a strange bird coming toward me out of the smoke. "That's the reason your grandma don't come to see me. She was always jealous. Used to preach to me 'bout my men but I knew what she was really thinking. She never had a figure like mine."

She leaned back into the chair, receded into the smoky haze. "When you want to go skinny-dippin', you come out here. Ain't never anybody around the lake. You come anytime you want. I won't be here but you just remember I was the one who told you to come. Now go on. Your ma's waitin'."

It was growing darker as we drove back, the sky a black wave falling on the long dreary warehouses. The streets, almost deserted, lay in wait for the rush hour that would soon begin.

"I know she looks awful," my mother was saying. "But she's old. When she was younger she was a . . . very . . . handsome woman. Very pretty."

"She said she had to get married," I said. "What did she mean?"

My mother looked at me and then looked quickly back at the road. "When did she say that?"

"When I went back in for the laundry."

"Well, she didn't mean anything. She was just rambling. Old people often don't know what they're saying."

I decided not to ask her about skinny-dipping, maybe because I had some vague sense of what the words meant. I had heard my brother use them. I fell silent and the sound of the words ran through my head over and over again.

I didn't get much time to brood over what I had seen and heard. That very night, just after we had eaten, there came a knock at the door and my mother opened it to Dr. Wiley, our preacher. I wasn't surprised. He had come one or two times before and I only wondered why my mother hadn't warned us, as she usually did. But when we all sat in a circle in the living room and the good preacher asked my father if he was sorry for his sins and I realized that Dr. Wiley had come to see my father, I was stunned.

For my father was not a religious man. This, in itself, was not unusual in a region in which the women looked after the family and religion and the men looked after business and themselves. But not only was my father not religious, he had no respect for religion or for preachers. And, most unusual of all, he voiced his disrespect from

time to time. Had he been a Catholic, he could have disliked priests—could even have disliked the church—and
still been a part of it. But for us religion was hundreds of
ad hoc spiritual encounters coming together on a Sunday
morning or during a revival week. And since there hasn't
been a born Catholic in my family since Henry VIII, my
father had no place to go on Sunday morning. By the time
my mother led my brother, my sister and myself out the
front door, he was sprawled on the sofa, his face covered
by a newspaper he had been reading, asleep.

"We're off to church!" my mother shouted at him.

Sometimes there was a grunt, sometimes there wasn't.

I suppose my father's hatred of religion was tied up
with his hatred of cemeteries; never have I known a man
who more abhorred them. My mother told me why: when
he was a small boy, he was surrounded by women—his
mother, aunts, cousins—who every Sunday, week after
week, year after year, took him on the long streetcar ride
to Westview Cemetery where he was forced to spend the
day wandering among the tombstones. Thus he came to
associate cemeteries not with death or heaven or hell but
with boredom. When he left school at the age of twelve
and went off with his father and brother to Miami to work
in the "boom," he swore he would never go to a cemetery
again and, except when his father and mother died, he
stuck by his oath.

But it wasn't only boredom. Listening to Aunt Hallie
and Aunt Mary and his mother year after year piously
proclaim the connection between a virtuous life and eternal bliss—and of course, the connection between a sinful
life and eternal damnation—probably led him to believe
in an unbreakable link between religion and death,
caused him to believe that religion tyrannizes through

fear. For him church and cemetery became one and somewhere along the line my father decided to stop thinking
about death. So rigidly did he abolish the ultimate reality
from his mind that, when death came, he was at first not
frightened by it but simply astounded. Only at the very
end did any trace of fear creep into his eyes. And possibly
at that moment his salvation seemed worth the indignity.

"Do you believe in Jesus Christ as your personal Lord
and Savior?" Dr. Wiley asked him, and my father, his eyes
fixed on the floor, answered, "Yes."

Exactly why he submitted to salvation I don't know.
Maybe my grandmother with her soup and her "advice"
and her seemingly endless search for her "stolen" shoe
drove him to it. Or maybe his hatred of graveyards
turned momentarily into fear and overwhelmed him. But
finally I don't think his conversion had anything to do
with death or with his mother. More likely it had to do
with his drinking.

I sometimes wonder which in the South came first,
fundamentalist religion or drinking. Both move to the
same rhythm: long dry spells broken by sudden binges.
Indeed, the similarity between the old-fashioned revival
and drunken sprees is striking. That was the way my
father drank, in intermittent bursts with great enthusiasm, knocking back the bourbon or blended whiskey
straight from the bottle or, in more refined moments
when he stood with the other men in the kitchen, in short
quick gulps from a shot glass. He drank to get drunk; that
was what drinking was for. If you were thirsty, you drank
iced tea or Coca-Cola. You kept your whiskey hidden, usually under the seat of your car. And when you started
drinking, you didn't stop until you were roaring drunk,
and often you didn't stop then but went on for days until
suddenly, mysteriously, you stopped, maybe because you

discovered, again and again, that whiskey can keep you from the mundane routine of life for only so long without actually taking you out of the world altogether.

Quite possibly, then, what lay behind that extraordinary living room prayer session was nothing more than timing—somehow my mother and the preacher came on the scene just when my father was due for a bender and rather than hitting the bars he hit the church several Sundays in a row. How strange it seemed, as we walked the block to the church, to have him with us, decked out in his suit and tie. How proud my mother was as she introduced him to her Sunday school class in front of the church after the service was over. How he must have struggled to stay awake during the interminable sermons. How ecstatic my mother must have been when, answering the call, he made his way to the front of the church where Dr. Wiley announced his salvation and asked the other members of the church to accept him. And I suspect that many people in the congregation were moved, believing that the family, the wife and children, had brought the erring father into the fold. All that remained to make the conversion complete was the baptism.

The Baptists practice total immersion. As they logically point out, "John didn't lead Jesus to the middle of a lake to sprinkle water on his head." In solid middle-class Atlanta the river or lake out behind the church had been replaced by the baptismal font, a small pool above and behind the preacher's podium and the choir. A couple of years earlier I had walked into the pool, placed my hands, one on top of the other, on my chest as I had been taught in rehearsal, and Dr. Wiley had grasped my hands with one of his, placed his other behind my back and lowered me into the water where, for one wild moment, I thought that he might drop me or hold me under too long. Then he hoisted me up and I struggled, half-blinded by the water, out of the pool. I had made it. But I was only nine years old at the time and weighed about a hundred pounds.

Now, in the darkened church, a single ray of light beaming on the pool, I watched my father, almost six feet tall and weighing close to 190 pounds and looking even larger in his white robe, wade to the center of the pool. He was larger than Dr. Wiley, and try as I might to get into the spirit of the occasion, to rejoice at my father's salvation, I could only pray, "O Lord, don't let Dr. Wiley drop him. Don't let Dad pull him under." It was one of the tensest moments of my life: my father crossed his hands on his chest, Dr. Wiley grasped them, shifted his own position to spread his legs and get more stability, then lowered my father into the water. "I baptise thee in the name of the Father and of the Son and of the Holy Ghost," he said. At least I know that is what he said; I didn't actually hear him because I could see that he was straining to hold on. It was a near thing. Dr. Wiley wavered and an image flashed through my head of Dr. Wiley plunging in after my father and the two of them floundering about, splashing water over the side of the pool. And, idiotically, the question ran through my head, Would that mean that Dr. Wiley had baptised himself as well? But that didn't happen. Dr. Wiley gathered his strength, gave a mighty heave and pulled my reborn father from the water, where he stood, water streaming out of his hair and over his blinking eyes until Dr. Wiley nudged him in the back to remind him to move along and make way for the pretty little girl who was already inching into the pool. I heaved a sigh. My father was born again. More important, he and Dr. Wiley had survived the delivery.

The only question was, would it last? We hoped for much and expected little. So little, in fact, that no more than a week later as I trudged up the front steps into the house and heard sobbing, I guessed that my father had fallen from grace already, that he was off on another bender. I had been trying to play basketball but the wind sweeping across the playground had kicked up dust that stung my face. I thought about going into the church but I remembered what had happened before, the crucified Christ staring down on the rows of empty pews. Finally, even though it was the day of the week that my mother went to see Minnie, anything seemed better than the bitter wind and I walked home.

When I entered the living room, I saw my mother sitting on the sofa, holding my grandmother in her arms. I asked her what was wrong, and she told me that Aunt Minnie had died. I didn't know what to say so I asked what people in movies always asked, "How? What happened?"

"She drowned. She fell in the lake and drowned."

My grandmother began to wail.

All night the wind rattled the windows and between gusts sleet ticked insistently against the glass. From time to time I heard the muffled voices of my parents downstairs and the sobs of my grandmother coming from the room down the hall. And Aunt Minnie's words—"I won't be here"—ran through my head over and over again.

Even though it was Saturday I woke a little earlier than usual. The house was strangely silent and dark and when I flicked the light switch, I discovered why: there was no electricity. My brother was still asleep. I looked into my grandmother's room and saw that she and my sister were also asleep. I crept downstairs, shivering in the cold air, and made my way to the kitchen, which I knew would be warm because of the gas range. Two empty plates stained with bacon grease and egg yellow were on the kitchen table, but the room, warm with the smell of gas and lit by a kerosene lamp, was empty. I heard noises in the basement and realized that my parents were probably trying to do something about the pipes that always froze because my father never got around to wrapping them. I noticed a newspaper lying next to the kerosene lamp. It had been folded into a square exposing a single item and I read the headline:

SOUTH FULTON WOMAN DROWNS

The opening paragraph gave the usual factual information but further down I read:

Whether or not the drowning was accidental or the result of [I paused over the unfamiliar word and pronounced it phonetically aloud] suicide has not been determined. Neighbors say Mrs. Shedd had been depressed for several months over the death of her son. One neighbor, Mr. Aaron Self, says he watched Mrs. Shedd walk to the edge of the lake.

"Then she just kept on walking, right out into the water," Mr. Self said. "I was about a hundred yards away. I started yelling but she never looked back. She just kept on walking. I ran as fast as I could to the lake, but by the time I got there she was already under water. There were some children playing near the lake, but they were all too little to do anything. They just shouted and pointed. I swam out and dove for her but I couldn't find her."

Police investigated the incident and found no evidence of foul play.

Suicide. What did the word mean? It sounded strangely familiar. I meant to ask may parents but when my mother came into the room, she saw the paper and snatched it away from me. And suddenly the light flickered on and off and then on. The refrigerator whirred and the radio hummed and came on, filling the room with popular music.

"Thank goodness for that," my mother said. "Now if we only had water. I swear, your father never does anything I ask him to."

I ate breakfast, put on several layers of clothes, pulled a wool cap over my ears and thick gloves over my hands and went outside. Everything—houses, trees, bushes, utility poles, telephone and electric wires—was covered with ice. Thick heavy ice that pulled the lower limbs of trees down to the earth. Though it had stopped sleeting, the sky was still overcast and dim and the ice was a gray-white glaze. Ice and trees and houses and sky seemed frozen into one enormous dull glow. As I walked, the ground in the front yard cracked beneath my feet.

I moved along the sidewalk carefully, slipping and sliding from time to time. Occasionally a car inched by. I passed the basketball court and managed to climb the hill to the corner where I stood by the cathedral and looked up and down Peachtree Street, which was a maze of cars turned sideways, backwards, jammed against the curb. An electric company truck weaved through them, making its way toward Peachtree Creek.

"I won't be here," she had said. But how could she know? Or did she just mean that she was old?

I turned and looked down the hill I had just climbed, at the frozen houses and trees lining either side of the suburban street, and wondered how anyone could walk into a lake in this kind of weather. I imagined my aunt in a black dress walking into the freezing water and walking farther and farther, as the man had said, the water rising to her knees, to her breasts, to her chin, finally to her stringy hair. And still she walked on the bottom of the lake. Was that what "suicide" meant? Walking out into a lake? No. That was "skinny-dipping." Suicide. Skinny-dipping. They couldn't be the same. And yet . . .

Suddenly the world was flooded with light. The sun broke through the overcast sky and the ice exploded into brilliant color. Trees glistened in bright whites and subtle blues, houses burned and wires were delicate threads of jewels criss-crossing the bushes that became gleaming cascades of ice. The beauty filled me with an inexpressible joy and I descended the hill slowly, carefully, moving toward my lawn at the bottom where redbirds were hopping about on tiny slivers of ice.

In the spring of that year, as my mother led my brother, my sister and me out the door on a Sunday morning, we passed my father, who was on the sofa sleeping off his religious bender, the newspaper spread over his face. "He had a hard week," she whispered. "We'll just let him sleep this morning." And we let him sleep the next Sunday morning. And the next . . .

His lapse didn't seem to bother my mother, probably because she figured that, having gotten on the fundamentalist rollercoaster with all its ups and downs, he at least had a chance. There was always the possibility that he would return to the fold. But whatever relationship he developed between himself and God during those months—if, indeed, he developed any relationship at all—had nothing to do with the church. The trouble was, the church contained nothing to hold him, nothing to sustain his conversion but Dr. Wiley's sermons (which I noticed he had already begun to sleep through without the benefit of sofa or newspaper), and not even a saint can sustain through willpower alone an extraordinary religious experience. As my father well knew, nature can transform grain into a liquid that takes a man out of himself, and a church that couldn't do more than that every Sunday couldn't hold him. Like all men he longed to discover the miraculous woven into the fabric of everyday life. What he discovered instead was a religion that conceived of life in terms of winning and losing and taught that ultimately earthly winning and losing depend not on forces outside our control but on ourselves. In other words, it was a religion that prepared one for everything but failure, so it couldn't lift him out of the world society had plunged him into, a world of bankers and loans and erratic weather in which he was doomed to lose whatever he gained. More important, it made it impossible for him to recognize true failure, to see that losing may be, in the great ritual of creation, but a part of success.

I was playing basketball on the Catholic church grounds. Basketball season was over and I was finishing my last year in elementary school. Already, in early April, the afternoons were hot, and after running up and down the court for awhile (and winning several national championships), I grew very thirsty. I rested the ball on the asphalt and walked across to the spigot in the wall of the school building. As I was bent over drinking, I thought I heard, above the rush of water, the unmistakable sound of a basketball being dribbled. When I looked up, sure enough someone had picked up my ball and was playing, or rather, trying to play, with it.

A nun.

I didn't know what to do. I stood and stared. Whether she was totally uncoordinated and hopelessly incompetent or whether the heavy folds of her habit so impeded her movement that she appeared to be, I couldn't tell. She couldn't sustain more than two bounces in a row and when she tried to shoot the ball, she grasped it in both hands, pulled it to her chest and pushed it harmlessly into the air. It sailed under the backboard, fell to the ground and rolled toward me. And then she saw me. She motioned, asking me to return the ball. I picked it up and carried it to the court.

"Is it yours?" she asked.

I nodded.

"Oh, yes, you're the one who plays here all the time."

And then I knew that she was the nun who often told me to leave — the tall ominous figure on the bank. But now she was no taller than I.

"Come on," she said. "Show me how."

Ludicrous as it was, I did my best to show her how to dribble and shoot. To this day I retain a vivid image of her trying to execute a jump shot: the small body straining to heave those enormous black robes, the weight of all her duties and obligations, off the ground. Finally, exhausted, she gave up.

"Well, it certainly isn't easy," she said. "How can you keep doing it for so long?"

As she asked the question, she ran her hand across her forehead in such a way that suddenly I realized she was a young woman, much younger than my mother. I was bewildered and angry at the same time, and before I knew it, I blurted out, "How do you know I'm not a Catholic?"

Naturally she was now the one who was bewildered. "What do you mean?"

"How do you know I'm not a Catholic? That's why you run me off, isn't it?"

Her look of bewilderment dissolved into the merest flicker of a smile. Then her expression became quite serious and it is only now, as I remember the event, that I know she was learning not to patronize. "No, no. That didn't have anything to do with it. It . . . it was the noise." She paused, seemed to make up her mind, and then went on. "Some of the older nuns found it . . . distracting. I mean, the noise of the ball bouncing disturbed them. That was all."

Her voice was soft, as soft as her eyes that rested on me lightly. And the day, the soft spring day, rested on me lightly. And maybe I remembered then what I remember now — my wild flight out of the cathedral, my father's hair falling over his water-streaked face. And then she leaned forward and handed me the ball and said, "It doesn't matter what you are. You can play here."

Maybe it was a miracle. I don't know. But it was the sweetest end of innocence one could imagine.

PART
2
1952-53

Logic and lust together
Come dimly tumbling down
And neither God nor non-God
Is either up or down.

— Louis MacNeice

Uncle Luther is lying on the glider on the front porch. I try to tiptoe by him, by the overpowering odor of what my father calls "Four Roses." I hear my name shouted in a whisper and when I turn, a finger motions me to the glider.

"Do you know the Fox Theater?" he asks.

"Yes."

"I did the plastering in it. Did you know that?"

"Yes."

"All the ornamental plastering. The foreman, he said, 'Luther, I only want you. Nobody else.' That's what he said."

And then a rambling tale of the Depression years when he was making "a hundred dollars a week, by God. A hundred dollars. I had to travel—Memphis, Charlotte, Jacksonville, Birmingham, Little Rock, everywhere. And everywhere I went there was all them men out of work. 'Course, Mimi didn't like my traveling, but I told her, 'Mimi, there's people who're starving 'cause they can't find any work.'"

The same tale over and over again. But my parents and my uncle tell another tale.

"A hundred dollars a week," says my mother. "And look at him now. He can't even hold a job."

"It was the army," my father says. "They ruined him. He was too old. They never should have taken him. Two years in the South Pacific."

Uncle Walter says, "I could have kept him out but he never told me till too late."

"Or if he and Mimi had had children. That's why Calvin didn't have to go."

"It would've ruined anybody, the things he saw."

"And he didn't drink before he went in. Not a drop."

But Luther never tells me any of this. He tells his own story. His face as red as his hair, he lies on the glider, stares at the ceiling of the porch and talks about his travels during the Depression, his work on the Fox Theater. And once, just before he disappears again, he reaches out, grabs my shirt, pulls me close, his lips almost against my ear, his voice reeking of the blended whiskey, and says, "You know, when I was in my working clothes, my overalls, Mimi wouldn't even speak to me. I'd pass her on the street and she'd look the other way. My own wife. Can you beat that?"

And then he roars with laughter.

-1-

In the summer of 1952 the benign smiling face of the leader was everywhere, the direct honest eyes of Father who turned a war machine into a great crusade that filled the Holy Land of Europe with farmboys and ghetto kids and wild and reckless college lads. And now the simple slogan was everywhere — on billboards, shop fronts, telephone poles, fire hydrants, on barns and country stores, omnipresent as Coca-Cola signs. City and country rejoicing in the great crusade accomplished, already reading the chronicles of the kind and gentle Father who saved the world, clamoring now for more salvation, chanting the slogan in the prosperity of a new and better world.

"This is your cousin Allen," my mother said.

I looked up and then I looked up again. There seemed to be no top to him. He smiled and his thin lips wrinkled beneath a bushy mustache.

"Six feet ten and a half," he said. He might as well have said one hundred feet.

His eyes registered a sad tenderness that contradicted the mustache. This was, after all, a time when no one had a mustache, when the line of hair beneath the nose still suggested Hitler. Many believed that Dewey had lost the election because people felt that you couldn't trust a man who had a mustache. But Allen's, which drooped at the edges just as his eyes drooped at the corners, seemed a part of the tenderness that bordered on weakness — seemed to suggest that if you couldn't trust him, it was because he couldn't trust himself.

But what made Allen so different was not his great height or his mustache — no, what make him different was that he had an existence outside the family that I could understand. He didn't sell cotton or build houses or paint

them or sell insurance; he played semi-pro basketball. My
mother told him that I played basketball, too. "They have
a real good team," she said. I winced and said quickly,
"It's only B team."

He smiled his thin weak smile again. "Nothing I like
more than amateur games. The players are more enthusiastic. There's more life in it."

I wanted to talk to him about hook shots and high and
low posts and zone defense, but I could only watch him
dissolve under the onslaught of my mother into a cousin
whose sister was another cousin, into the son of a great-
uncle who was a security guard for a large factory in East
Point. He became just another relative and by the time he
rose to leave I was lost in thoughts of getting away.

"What was your record?" he asked.

The question brought me back into the room and
Allen was a basketball player again. "Eighteen and two,"
I said.

He whistled softly through his mustache. "I guess I'll
have to come and see you play."

"Why haven't I seen him before?" I asked after he
had left.

"Because he left home when he wasn't much older
than you, only sixteen or so. I know because he tried to
join the army. It was during the war but they wouldn't
have him."

"Because he was too young."

"No, he was old enough by then. It was something
else . . . it doesn't matter. Anyway, he didn't go back
home. It broke his mother's heart."

"Where did he go?"

"Who knows? All over. California, Chicago. Finally he
turned up in New Orleans, working on the docks or

something. Since he doesn't even have a high school education, he can't get a good job."

Maybe he broke his mother's heart, but for me he
became the man who escaped, got away to strange places.
I imagined him as one of the men in Sam's Bar, a place I
was too young to go into. All I could do was stand outside
and peer into its mysterious dark interior until I could
make out the shapes of the men sitting at the semi-
circular bar. They sat on high barstools, their feet planted
on the crossbraces, their elbows propped on the counter.
I couldn't see their faces but I was dimly aware of eyes
and slightly open mouths. And I knew that they were not
wearing ties. But most of them had on hats, hats pushed
back on their heads. And the smoke curling up from the
cigarettes they held between the fingers of the hand
wrapped around the bottle added to the darkness. They
were men I had seen photographs of in books—men in
heavy wrinkled clothes and battered shoes, leaning
against old black cars, scrawny dogs at their feet, smiling
or maybe just squinting at the sun that had to be at the
back of whoever was taking the picture. Strangers. I
didn't know where they came from. Maybe they were
passing through.

It wasn't that I didn't have any contact with the world
outside my world. Ever since I could remember, once a
week in the afternoon Mr. Castleberry's battered green
pickup truck pulled to a stop in front of our house. He
had wonderful things in the back of that truck: butter,
white and round, and brown eggs in square flats, both—
butter and eggs—always cool to touch, even in the heat of
summer. And sometimes there were cabbages and sometimes bright orange carrots or shiny yellow squash (I wondered how things could look so splendid and taste so

awful). Mr. Castleberry smelled of his produce or his produce smelled of him. It didn't matter. He, his truck, his butter and eggs and his vegetables were all one to me.

"Where does he come from?" I asked my mother.

"From the country," she said.

And for a long time that was enough. It never occurred to me to ask where in the country because there wasn't any "where." The country was . . . the country, a place just outside Atlanta. It was from that place that my grandmother, my mother's mother, and many of her eighteen or nineteen brothers and sisters had come. To hear my grandmother and my great-aunts and -uncles talk about it, "the country" was another world, so different from my own that it had to be far away. But it wasn't. Mr. Castleberry could drive back and forth between those worlds in a day, in less than a day.

Of course, I had been to "the country." You had to pass through it if you went anywhere on vacation and from time to time I had even been to Rowena, where my grandmother came from. But it always drifted by outside the car window, so separate from me that I might as well have been back in my house in Buckhead. And at Rowena, when I actually got out of the car and stepped into "the country," I found it to be a threatening place, full of ferocious chickens and huge cows.

But certainly Mr. Castleberry's red wrinkled face, his gnarled hands, his overalls and brogans didn't seem hostile or threatening. And there was that other marvelous thing he brought into my world — his voice. Slow and deliberate, it spoke a language so strange — so "ungrammatical" — I could hardly make out what he said yet what I did make out were words as solid as his truck, words you could touch like you could touch his eggs or his butter.

And so, when, soon after Allen came and went, one of my grandmother's sisters fell ill and we took my grandmother to Rowena to see her, I didn't think much of it. I had been to Rowena before, but those other trips had left only vague impressions. And my other grandmother, Kate, stood on the front porch as we were getting ready to leave, jealous that we would go to visit someone else. "Go off to see Lena and leave me here by myself. Anything could happen to me."

"We've asked you to come with us."

"It's all right," she muttered. And then she said what I had been hearing her say ever since I could remember, "You'll miss me when I'm dead and gone."

It was early spring and still cold when we left the city, and the rolling farmland, poor country at best back then, seemed as vast and as dead as the gray sky. I sat in the back seat and stared out at the empty land that flowed by. Barren cotton fields, being taken over by scrawny second-growth timber, stretched to the horizon in all directions. From time to time there flashed by a weather-beaten shack leaning crazily to one side or an old barn that had fallen into a heap of rotting timber or a rusty metal-sided cotton gin, its windows boarded up. The small towns we passed through seemed about as desolate as the countryside and the desolation was made more acute by an occasional solitary man trudging along by the side of the road. Where is he going? I wondered. Where has he come from?

The house smelled of damp earth and coal and kerosene and the rough board walls were covered with old sepia photographs and faded Victorian landscapes framed in gaudy tarnished gilt. It was Sunday and relatives and neighbors had come by after church still dressed in their best clothes. They milled about, talking of politics and the weather and the economy: the same big-boned, red-faced men and women I had seen at the family reunions in Piedmont Park in Atlanta only there they seemed almost quaint, picturesque. Here they were a part of the grim land, closing in on me. I clung desperately to whatever differences I could find: my city clothes fit, my father was a builder, my mother bought her clothes at Rich's and played bridge. I wasn't a part of this world; I was merely a visitor, passing through. Whenever I could, I looked out the window at our new car, the one that would carry me back to the city.

My mother took me into the bedroom to see my great-aunt. I leaned over and kissed the gaunt face on one sunken cheek.

"Is this your boy, Margaret?"

My mother nodded. "Yes. Well, one of them. The younger."

"My goodness, I don't think I've ever seen him before. He looks just like Homer."

I was surprised that she could speak. I had assumed that she was dying though actually she was no more death-like than many of the women in the next room. Still, the words coming out of her mouth seemed more solid than the body.

"Go get your father," my mother said after we were back in the living room.

"Where is he?"

She looked at me, her face filled with disgust. "You know where he is."

So I went back to the kitchen and found him standing at the sink, drinking with some of the other men. When I told him that Mother wanted to see him, he made a face, raised the small glass to his mouth and knocked back what was left in it.

As we entered the living room, we almost bumped into a boy who was about my age.

"Well, who are you?" my father asked.

"Homer."

"Homer? Homer who?"

"It's Cora's boy, Lena's grandson," my mother, who had come up to us, said. "You wouldn't remember."

His navy blue suit—threadbare, obviously handed down for years from brother to brother—was too small for him and his hands and wrists stretched well below the ends of the sleeves, just as his brogans and white socks high above his ankles were exposed. The suit coat strained at its buttons and the clumsy knot of his tie hung to one side. His face was as weathered as a man's and his hands were already scarred. "Well, your Aunt Lena was right," my mother said. "He certainly does look like you." And I thought desperately, *No. No, he doesn't.*

But when we left, when I got to the car and was about to get in, I looked back at the house and saw him standing on the porch, looking at us. His face was my face, his eyes were my eyes, staring back at me. I looked away, then looked back. I was still there, staring at myself, but gradually—I couldn't break free, couldn't turn my head again—my face dissolved and it was his face again, his eyes, locked on mine now, pulling me to him, pulling me back to the house. And all at once I knew what I had feared and I struggled to break the grip of his eyes before they pulled me back into that bedroom.

But the eyes remained. On the trip back they stared at me out of the darkening landscape. Even as we entered the city my fear didn't go away. Atlanta, like my great-aunt, was the center of a circle; all around it, just beyond the suburbs, lay the dead farmland. True, highways and rails connected it with the great cities outside the South—

New York, Chicago, Los Angeles—but you had to get on those roads and ride through the dead land to break free.

I felt those eyes when, two or three days later, my father and my uncles fell once again to raging against "the county unit system."

"Hell, three counties in south Georgia with a combined population of 6000 can outvote the whole city of Atlanta."

"Rednecks" and "hicks" and "plowboys" and "crackers," all inhabitants of "the country," ran the state, it seemed, by electing those small-town lawyers who came to Atlanta once a year "to get drunk and raise hell and do whatever Old Gene or some other redneck tells 'em to do." Old Gene, Eugene Talmadge, had been dead for years, but he still epitomized everything awful about "the country." He had, in the ultimate symbolic gesture, set a cow out to graze on the lawn of the governor's mansion in Ansley Park, one of the most fashionable sections of the city.

The relatives who talked that way were my city relatives, for while one side of my family, my mother's side, had come up from the country, my father came from town people—painters and carpenters and glaziers and plasterers and bricklayers—some of whom had risen into the business world. In fact, my father was born in the city, which made me a second generation Atlantan. And I felt in his words a scorn for the country, utterly devoid of any pity for all those people in Rowena.

For me, though, unless I wanted to ride the bus or go with my parents, "the city," like the country, was far away. What I knew was Garden Hills, a few buildings strung along Peachtree Road that you passed just before you came to Buckhead. The liquor store owner, a Yankee with an unpronounceable Italian name, stood in the doorway and had a smile and a kind word for every passerby. He seemed unaware that on Sunday mornings two blocks down the street Dr. Wiley preached against the evils of his trade. A few doors down from the liquor store was Abraham's Delicatessen, where you could sit at a table covered with a red and white checkered cloth and eat a sandwich piled high with paper thin roast beef. Like the liquor store owner, Abraham was a "foreigner."

Mr. Cobb—fat, red faced, a cigar always protruding from his mouth—ran Cobb's Food Store; his competition was a slight, oddly refined little man named Shuman, who ran the other grocery store on the block. There were also a small movie house, a barber shop and beauty salon (run by husband and wife), a record shop with glass booths where you could play your records before you bought them, a filling station and Sam's Bar. And Carter's Drugstore where Dr. Carter, a bald, immaculately dressed man (he always wore a suit with a vest and gold watch chain, even in the dead of summer), sat at the back of the store, one hand—carefully manicured—resting on the round bentwood table in front of him, and watched the world with a cynical eye while above his head a long-bladed wooden ceiling fan turned in slow silent circles. I worked for him one summer and for three months felt his eyes on me. Occasionally he would rise, pad silently across the tile floor, seize one of the ice cream cartons I had filled and take it back to his apothecary scales. If it weighed over a certain amount he would lecture me once again on profit margins. And when any of my friends came to the soda fountain for an ice cream or a Coke, I could feel his eyes peering out from among the shelves of medicine, watching me to make sure I didn't give anything away.

And there were the blacks, those who worked in the grocery stores and filling station, who leaned against the buildings or stood at the bus stop. They were like the solitary men I had seen trudging by the side of deserted highways: I didn't know where they came from or where they went. It never occurred to me that they—and Abraham and the Italian Yankee and Shuman and the others—had lives independent of the buildings. They and the low slung block of concrete and brick shops made up the Garden Hills I passed through every morning on my way to school, rode my bicycle to several times a day in the summer on errands for my mother and grandmother. It was a world that existed only in the daylight. And the dark cave-like interior of Sam's bar, Dr. Carter's shiny head and clipped fingernails, the summer sun reflecting off the storefronts were all one with the dogwood tree in my front yard, with the old basketball court.

That summer my mother decided that I was too old to have so much time on my hands, and especially when I began to use that time to see Vicki—or rather, to try to see her—then my mother came to agree with my grandmother that "an idle mind is the devil's workshop" and insisted that I take a paper route. Even at the time, I wondered how delivering papers was going to keep me from evil thoughts and I resisted for awhile, but when my father declared that "he's too old to be playing with a chemistry set," I knew I couldn't win. How could I tell him that I wasn't playing with the chemistry set, that it had been over two years since I exploded a test tube and put the stain on the ceiling that is still there. Now my chemistry set was simply an excuse to examine my curious object.

It was small, smaller even than most marbles, had a rough, reddish-brown surface and was hard as a pebble. I don't know how it got into the chemistry set but I didn't doubt that it was what I had been told it was, though I couldn't remember who told me. It was a mystery of science: like chairs which were actually billions of little spinning balls, this object was not what, in its ordinary surroundings, it appeared to be, but smaller and harder. I kept it wrapped in an old cloth and hidden behind a row of bottles on the top shelf; I examined it under the microscope only when I knew I wouldn't be surprised by my mother or my father, who were sure to know what it was.

So I had to take the paper route, which meant that on Sundays I had to get up before dawn and pedal my bicycle to Garden Hills, and in the darkness of that hour—when there were no people on the sidewalks and no cars on the streets, when nothing was moving but myself and the only sounds were my own breathing and the slap of newspapers against porches—my daylight world dissolved and the shops in Garden Hills seemed to come to life, to breathe, even to move. Then I realized that those buildings existed independent of me, that when I wasn't there, they were. But it was more than that: not only when I wasn't there, but when Mr. Cobb wasn't there either. Or Mr. Shuman. Or Mr. Carter. When I was asleep only the buildings were there, standing in the dark: the vegetables beneath the sheets, the quarts of ice cream in the freezer, the bottles of whiskey and wine. The very bricks, their red brilliance turned sullen by the glow from the streetlamps fading in the rising light, seemed alive, responding to the outer world. And my reflection in the glass storefronts was a dark image, a ghost pedaling beside me. To cover my fear I tried to conjure up the amiable Italian Yankee, old Abraham, red-faced cigar-smoking Mr. Cobb, friends and neighbors going in and out of the shops.

But I couldn't escape this world within a world, couldn't blot it out of my mind, mainly because stretching along the other side of Peachtree was the Slaton estate, a large house so obscured by acres of wooded land that it could only be glimpsed from the road in the winter when the trees were bare. And surrounding the property was a high fence. Rumor had it that a pack of dogs — German Shepherds or Dobermans — roamed the grounds, and though I never saw them I often heard howls and I certainly imagined them — large beasts with white teeth that gleamed in the moonlight. As I moved along the other side of Peachtree, I glanced furtively across the street and wondered if the dogs could get over the fence.

But I was all right so long as I perceived no connection between those day and night worlds, so long as my Sunday morning ride was a descent into a strange place, an alien country I rode into and out of. All I had to do was stick to the path I knew and inevitably daylight would come and wipe out that other country. I still believed in such a fantasy, believed in the separation between night and day, between past and present.

For it was a time of fantasy. Even in broad daylight I could plunge into the darkness of the Garden Hills Theater and watch John Wayne, who was still shooting up the slant-eyed devils. After all, the Korean "police action" was a reminder of that crusade. Our feelings about war were mixed. The idea of going into combat if the Korean conflict dragged on until we were eighteen frightened us, but uniforms and rifles and marching were mixed up in our feelings with sex: we believed that soldiers were irresistible to women and though we never said it to each other, we longed for a world divided between warriors and their women.

Fantasies twisted and turned around one another like snakes: fugitives, long roads winding through strange lands, escapes from our world, from ourselves. Even before I began to taunt Vicki with my curious object I had begun to weave all my imaginings into an elaborate construct of escape. Cousin Allen only fed an obsession that already existed, an obsession with routes and maps. Even now, when the nights stretch endlessly before me, I counter their dark distances with my memories of journeys. I recall vividly the exact route my family took from our home in Atlanta to Florida thirty-five years ago: US 41 to Barnesville, US 341 to Perry, US 41 to Lake City, US 100 to Bunnell, US 1 to Daytona Beach. Then I'm in the back seat of the Chrysler coupe or the Hudson Hornet; my head leans against the window and the countryside rolls by, mile after mile, until the steady rhythm of trees and signboards and roadside stores and filling stations and cows and leaning shacks rocks me into dreams.

I seldom remembered the dreams. But then, I don't remember many of the places we stayed at on those summer vacations thirty years ago. Or what we did. I remember the sea, of course, but it's as though the roads I traveled, like my distant memory of them, lulled me into sleep and forgetfulness. And then, on a rainy winter day when I'm driving through the town I live in now and my son asks me what Spanish moss is, suddenly I see the clump that hung on the lower limb of the dogwood tree in front of my house. It was as out-of-place in that Atlanta suburb as a palm tree or a black family would have been yet no one seemed to notice or remark on it; and a few days after I hung it there, even I had forgotten about it. Which seems strange when I consider how it got there.

I suppose I get my own obsession with routes and maps from my father. He could — and on the slightest provocation would—tell you how to get from Pascagoula to Birmingham or from Hahira to Pulaski, complete with all detours and shortcuts. Moreover, he could tell you how long it took to get from town to town; and once he had you hooked, he would start in on his records: "The fastest I ever made it from Gainesville to Opelika was . . ." or "I once drove from Memphis to St. Augustine without stopping for anything but gas." It was this last record, and the endurance it involved, that tormented my family through all my childhood.

While I was still a child, and for a long time afterwards, I thought that my father's obsession with roads, with getting from one place to another, was a conditioned response, that the job he had during the Depression— traveling for Sears, remodeling and installing mail order stores—was a job he took because during the Depression one took *any* job. It never occurred to me that he might not even have cared about getting from one place to another, that there might have been another explanation, another reason why, when he arranged jobs in Florida in the summer and took the family on vacation while he worked, he was incapable of changing his attitude.

My mother knew what to expect and tried to prepare for it, much as Arabs must prepare for trips across the desert, but there were six of us in the family—myself, my mother and father, my brother and sister and my grandmother—so there wasn't much room for provisions. There wasn't much room in the car for anything but feet and legs and shoulders. My father filled up the tank the night before the trip, we ate breakfast in the dark and left at dawn, "to beat the traffic." Mother never ceased to be hopeful. "Maybe we can do some sightseeing along the way," she suggested. "We're leaving so early, we don't have to hurry." And always my father was very agreeable and at the beginning of every trip he vowed to stop at the Stephen Collins Foster Museum or Cypress Gardens or Silver Springs. I think he even intended to; he was basically a good-hearted man. But a highway was to him what whiskey is to an alcoholic.

So this journey, like all the others, started pleasantly enough. More pleasantly, in fact, since I wouldn't have to deliver papers for two weeks and since I had begun to think of the beach not as a place of fierce waves and sandcastles but in terms of girls: girls on the sand and girls on the boardwalk; girls in the dark game rooms, their slim arms propelling the ski-balls, their hips moving with the silver balls in the pinball machines. They danced in my head as we passed through Barnesville and Fort Valley and Perry and the great expanses of peach orchards. They sustained me when the land began to flatten, the sun rose higher in the sky and the damp morning air gave way to the blistering heat of south Georgia. All the windows were rolled down and the hot wind that swirled through the car couldn't even dry the sweat that rolled down our foreheads and bodies. But the thought of those girls, of their golden hair and their smooth tanned skin and their long legs, kept me from the reality of the car for awhile longer. Finally we began to shift about, trying to get our legs in new positions, bumped into one another and squabbled. My grandmother told us to stop fighting.

"Let's stop and stretch our legs and get a Coke," my mother said.

My father stared ahead, one sunburned arm hanging out the window as he clutched the steering wheel with a hand that held a cigarette wedged between two fingers, the ashes blowing into the back seat from time to time, and said nothing.

"Look," she said, pointing to a roadside sign. "There's a Stuckey's in ten miles. Let's stop there."

Our spirits rose as the signs rolled by: Stuckey's 8 Miles; Stuckey's 6 Miles; Stuckey's 3 Miles; Stuckey's 1 Mile.

"There it is," Mother said.

"I can't stop now. I'd have to pass all those trucks again."

And Stuckey's, filled with happy people drinking Coca-Colas and orange juice, flew by. I turned and, much as Lot's wife must have looked wistfully back before she turned into a pillar of salt, watched it fade behind us. We could deceive ourselves no longer. Our only hope now was the gas tank. From the back seat I peered over my father's shoulder and watched the needle on the gas gauge fall. It was like watching the hour hand on a clock.

"I have to go to the bathroom," said my sister.

"So do I," said my brother.

"I'm thirsty," I chipped in.

"Calvin," my grandmother said sternly. "We must stop at the next filling station. Elizabeth has to go to the bathroom."

"All right."

The next filling station "probably didn't have a bathroom." The next one was "too dirty." We crossed the Georgia-Florida line. My mother stared out the window, her face filled with despair as my grandmother told us that "Calvin's always been this way. Even when he was a little boy he was stubborn as a mule."

"It looks like we'll make Lake City in six hours," my father announced, his voice filled with excitement. "And we're getting good gas mileage."

I peered over his shoulder once again. The needle had fallen to the quarter tank mark. My stomach rumbled with hunger and my kidneys ached. Over the car there fell a deadly silence that lasted mile after flat hot Florida mile. We gave up pointing to filling stations; signs announcing the small towns we passed through meant no more than the "Come Again" signs that flashed by soon after. The turnoff to the Stephen Collins Foster Museum came and went like a half-remembered dream. Our only hope was the car, which, unlike my father, had its limits. Or so I thought.

"Calvin, the gas gauge is on empty."

"We can make it to Lake City," he shot back as we passed a sign that read, "Lake City 17 Miles."

I fixed my eyes on the odometer and watched the numbers tick off: 16, 15, 14, 13. Then I gave up; it was hopeless. We would never get to Lake City. We would never get anywhere. We were doomed to die in a car that never stopped moving because, miraculously, it never ran out of gas. My brother groaned, my sister was rolled up in a tight ball, Grandmother's eyes were glazed, my mother put her arms on the dashboard and rested her head on them. And the last thing I remember seeing before I closed my own eyes was my father, cool and determined, staring straight ahead. Without doubt he would drive straight through the state of Florida and on to the South Pole.

"Calvin, please," my mother moaned. "We're on vacation."

I collapsed into a hot blackness.

"Lake City."

A sound, far in the distance. No. My father's triumphant voice. I looked up and before me, swimming in my sticky, sweat-filled eyes, stretched a wide street lined on either side with filling stations. I didn't believe it at first but when my father said, "We made it," I knew I wasn't dreaming. Then he said, "Let's find a good one," and my heart sank; as far as I could tell, there was no such thing as a good filling station.

But then the car began to sputter and jerk.

"What the hell?"

My mother lifted her head from her arms. "Gas," she mumbled. "We're out of gas."

And my father, muttering angrily, steered the car into a filling station.

I sometimes wonder what the attendants at the station thought when they saw a medium-priced late model car die before a gas pump and then explode. All doors flew open and we tumbled out and made a dash for the restrooms. My brother and I ran side by side. I threw a glance back at my sister, who was hunched over and limping toward the women's room, my mother next to her, helping her along. Only my grandmother retained her dignity. She stepped slowly from the car, rose to her full height, straightened her hat, swept the wrinkles from her black skirt and glared at her son for a moment.

But he already had the map spread on the hood of the car and was studying the route for the remainder of the journey. Of course, he knew the route; he knew how to get from Lake City to anywhere in the South. But there he was, off the road but still on it, traveling it with his finger, lost in relentless movement and the hum of the engine, oblivious to the desperate orgy of his family as it emerged from the restrooms, descended upon the office and gulped down soft drinks and pumped money into the candy machines. "Buy anything you want," my mother said grimly as she dispensed nickels. "This is our only chance." We came out of the office loaded down with peanut butter crackers, moonpies, candy bars and soft drinks. The stunned attendant came to his senses long enough to say, "Hey, lady, you got to pay for those bottles if you take them with you."

"It's all right!" my father shouted. He was refolding the map, anxious to get started. "We'll stop for drinks down the road."

My mother glared at him for a moment, then said to the attendant, "How much?" He could have said, "A dollar a bottle," and it wouldn't have mattered.

"Okay, let's get going," my father said. He was back behind the wheel and, clutching our provisions, we wedged back into the car. The doors were still closing as we roared away from the pump. In horror, we realized that he was trying to get to the highway ahead of a truck that was nearing the station. "No, Calvin, we can't make it!" my mother shouted and at the last moment he slammed on the brakes. The truck roared by and he muttered, "Damn. Now I'll have to pass him again."

As the car pulled onto the highway, I looked out the back window and saw the attendants standing in front of their ransacked station and staring at us in utter bewilderment. Slowly they faded, became specks in the distance and disappeared. "A hundred and eighty-seven miles to go," my father said. "If we don't hit too much traffic we'll make it by four o'clock." He swung the car out into the oncoming lane and repassed the truck. "I think that was the only one," he said.

We all settled back, looked out the window at the Spanish moss trailing from the limbs of the trees, fingered our crackers and candy and drinks, and tried not to think of the miles that lay between us and the beach. The worst was over. One way or another we would survive.

I think it was then, as I was slumped in the seat, my head resting against the window, my eyes fixed on the monotonous flat wasteland that stretched as far as the eye

could see in all directions—a desolation between the
squat stolid suburbs of Atlanta and that other stretch of
endless reality, the sea—I think it was then that the words
leaped out of the bewildering maze of billboards that
lined either side of the road. Billboards advertising
oranges and grapefruits and lemons and orange juice and
beach towels and suntan lotion and . . . papaya juice.
Papaya. I had seen the word on previous trips; I even
knew how to pronounce it. But I had seen Spanish moss
before, too. Only now the two merged, the mysterious
sound echoing in my head through dark mysterious forests draped with the grey hanging plant.

Explain it any way you like: adolescent fantasy, igno-
rance, exhaustion, the desire to escape the car and the
family I was trapped in. Whatever, the word came to rep-
resent all the exotica of the tropics—rain forests and
strange animals and thatch huts beneath the burning sun.
Every time the word appeared beside the road I saw
myself as a traveler moving through the lush sun-
drenched colors of countries whose names I could hardly
pronounce. They were all somewhere *south*, farther south
than Florida, farther south even than Cuba and Haiti.
That's where papaya (whatever it was) came from. At
times I was sure I could smell it, a rich pungent odor, like
that of overripe oranges with a hint of banana mingled in.
But different.

That night as I lay on the screened porch of our cottage and listened to the surf, I pronounced the word over
and over again until I strolled along another beach, a
semicircle of soft white sand embracing water so clear I
could see the small brightly colored fish swimming in it.
And behind me as I walked a deep green jungle stretched
to the mountains that loomed dark in the distance. At first
I walked by myself, a lonely brooding man, but gradually

there emerged beside me another figure — vague, shadowy — that made me tremble with emotion.

By day the beach came to lose all its charm. I had no desire to tumble with the younger children in the breakers and I was disgusted by the motels and hot dog and raft rental stands that stood between the sea and the road. Ski-ball was boring; the chicken that danced when I put a nickel in the slot wasn't funny; even the pinball machines — an old obsession — didn't interest me. There were the girls, of course, their tanned skin bulging against their tight bathing suits, but they roamed the beach in giggling packs, moving fortresses that could be assaulted only by packs of boys as loud and aggressive as they. A loner like myself had no chance. I could only watch them from a distance or stroll casually by them as they lay stretched on the sand and cast furtive sidelong glances at their bodies. They were what I had come to the beach for; they were exactly as I had imagined them in Atlanta, in the car. And now, surrounded by them, I found myself drifting away although my heart still pounded when I imagined my hands touching their flesh.

"What's wrong with you?" my mother asked. "You don't seem to be having any fun."

But I couldn't explain to her how the word *papaya* had altered my life. I couldn't even explain it to myself, anymore than I could explain why I refused to drink papaya juice. It was sold everywhere but for two weeks I held back, pronounced the word over and over again but refused to drink it.

Maybe she said something to my father, told him something was wrong with me. How else account for his turning up at the beach in the middle of the afternoon? Since arriving I had seen him only in the early morning

when he left for work and late in the afternoon, sometimes after dark, when he came back to the cottage, ate
and went to bed. Now he stood on the beach, and had he
been a pine tree he couldn't have looked more out of
place in his tie and dark pants and heavy leather shoes.

"How are you doing?" he asked.

"Fine."

He stared out at the sea.

"Are you all right?"

"Yeah. Sure. How come you're not at work?"

He hesitated. "We're almost finished. I could take a
little time off."

"Oh."

He looked at me, started to say something, then
turned his eyes back out to the sea. "Just think," he said,
"if you keep going out that way," he pointed to the horizon, "you'll hit . . . what? Africa? Europe?"

"Africa, I think."

He looked down, kicked the sand. "Boy, it's hot. How
do you stand it?"

I didn't answer.

"Well, I just wanted to make sure you're having a
good time." He hesitated again, looked at me for a
moment, then turned his eyes down the beach. "I've got
to get back."

"Okay."

He walked toward the road but when he got to the
dunes he turned and shouted, "You look out for the
girls!" and laughed.

"I will!" I shouted back.

That evening my mother asked me, "Did your father
talk to you today?"

"Yes."

"What did he say?"

"Oh, nothing much. The usual, you know. He asked me if I was having a good time."

"And that's all?"

"More or less."

She was standing at the sink, her back to me as she washed dishes. "He wishes he could spend more time with you. But he has to work so hard. It hasn't been easy for him. He had to quit school in the seventh grade. When you consider that, it's amazing what he's done." She stared into the dishwater much as he had stared at the sea. "He's a good man. He'd do anything for you."

"I know."

But what did I know? My mother always brought up my father's lack of education, as though that explained everything, but I didn't know what there was about my father to be explained. Moreover she seemed to find great significance in what was simply the routine of our lives, a routine I never questioned because nothing else seemed possible. And when my father came in after dark with a slight smell of bourbon on his breath and complained about how badly the job was going, the routine seemed as unbreakable as ever.

As the two weeks passed and the girls faded farther and farther beyond my reach, my shadowy companion took shape—or rather *she* for it was most certainly a *she*, formed and dissolved beside me over and over again. Sometimes she was tall, dark and willowy; sometimes she was petite, fair and delicate. But always her breasts were the same: impossibly erect, large and at once firm and soft (though I never touched them; they merely brushed against my arm from time to time as we strolled along the beach).

On the night before we left I couldn't sleep, haunted as I was by the fear that I had gotten halfway to a place I would never see. To the north lay Atlanta, my brick house on East Wesley Road, the steam radiators that would hiss through the winter, North Fulton High School, its dingy halls and classrooms. To the south lay my dream of paradise, a dream growing from the smells of sea and sand, smells the gaudy trappings of Daytona—the neon lights and cars and the stench of hamburgers—couldn't obliterate. I got up, tiptoed out of the cottage, eased the screen door shut behind me, and made my way over the dunes to the beach. A half moon hung low in the sky and sent streaks of pale light along the shifting surface of the sea, light that rose and shattered on the sand with the waves. The stars in the heavens, the sound of the surf, the rippling moonlight. Yet there was nothing I could touch, could feel. No, not even the woman who stood beside me—as solid and distant as the stars, as solid and ephemeral as the sound of the waves. To come so close . . .

And then it rushed away, flew backward as the car hurtled forward through dreary flat stretches of land toward Lake City. Farther and farther away. The car encapsulated the world that lay ahead: my brother fretted about missing the first day of football practice, my sister clung to her stuffed donkey and struggled against car sickness, my grandmother pontificated on the evils of the modern world, the immorality of the beach and the almost naked women.

I panicked. Everything was fading, vanishing forever. Papaya was my only hope, a miserable hope offered by a small sign stabbed into the sand by the side of the road. "All the Orange juice U Can drink 25." And below that, among "Cantaloupes, Grapefruit, Lemons, Limes," buried among them, the last letters squeezed against the edge of the sign, "Papaya juice." I pronounced the word aloud. "Papaya."

"What?" my mother asked.

"Papaya juice. The next place has papaya juice. I want to stop."

"We just started," my father said. Actually we had been on the road for over an hour.

"I don't care," I whined, a little ashamed because my voice was like that of a six year old. "I want to stop."

"We'll stop at the next place."

"That's what you always say. And you never stop. I want to stop at *this* place!" By now I was shouting, and even my brother, who never noticed anything, was looking at me. And so was my mother. *What is it*? her eyes asked. How could I answer? What could I say?

"Please stop, Calvin," she said. "It won't take but a minute. We'll just let him jump out and jump back in."

"Stop for papaya juice. He's had two weeks to drink papaya juice. Damn it, I wanted to make . . ."

"Please." She lowered her voice. "Can't you see there's something wrong? Please."

He looked at me in the rearview mirror. "All right. I'll stop for two minutes. That's all. Understand?"

He pulled the car off onto the sandy parking area in front of a small sagging fruitstand, behind the center of which stood an enormous fat woman who was swatting flies off herself and the fruit stacked in front of her.

"Okay, now the rest of you stay in . . ."

But already all the doors were open. Nobody was going to miss what might be our only chance for hours.

On one side of me stood my brother, gulping down glass after glass of orange juice; on the other side of me my sister was telling my mother that she was sick and

needed a bathroom; behind me my grandmother complained about how filthy the fruitstand was; my father sat
behind the steering wheel and stared grimly ahead. And
on the counter in front of me stood my small cup of
papaya juice. I had no way of understanding what I felt at
that moment. Only years later when I read Keats, especially the line, "O for a beaker full of the warm South,"
would I experience some understanding of that feeling. I
reached out, raised the cup to my mouth and drank.

The sticky sweet taste was revolting. It oozed about
my mouth, caught halfway down my throat and almost
made me gag. I stared at the cup and, unable to withstand another swallow, I pronounced the word *papaya*
aloud.

"What is it?" my mother asked. "Don't you like it?"

The word that had held such promise, had transformed the dreary world around me, now became a part
of that world, as disgusting as my gluttonous brother, my
whining sister, my overbearing grandmother. But before I
could answer, my father, who had bolted from the car,
was upon us, flapping his arms and shouting. "Come on!
We've got to get back on the road! Hurry up!"

I wandered away from the group, off to the edge of a
little clearing. Behind me I could hear my father haggling
with the fat woman.

"He gave some of it to the others," she said. "Nobody
could drink that much orange juice."

"The hell he did. Your sign says all you can drink for a
quarter, and that's all I'm paying."

There stretched before me, as far as I could see, trees
draped with Spanish moss. The taste of papaya juice that
still lingered in my mouth clashed with my vision of the
trees, gloomy and mysterious. I recalled what I had felt
two weeks before when the Spanish moss first loomed

before me. I wandered in among the trees and — without really knowing what I was doing — I began pulling handfuls of it from the lower branches and stuffing it in my pockets. The feel of it against my hand seemed to take the taste from my mouth and, obsessed, I filled my pockets and piled it in my arms. I would carry it back with me, carry the paradise it foretold back to Atlanta.

My family had gathered in a semicircle around the fat woman. She was threatening to call the state police, my father was threatening to sue her, my mother was trying to pull my father away and my brother was shouting, "I didn't give any away! I drank it all myself!"

I stuffed the moss under the front seat and between the cushion and the back of the rear seat. And I kept a small clump clutched tightly in my fist. A talisman, a charm against the world.

We were well into middle Georgia before my sister began to complain of itching. My own arms had been itching for quite a while but I had hardly noticed it, so caught up was I in my own visions. Then my grandmother began to scratch her legs. Soon everyone was scratching and cursing. "What is it?" my mother asked. The car swerved as my father tried to scratch and drive.

"What's this?" My brother, who had reached down to scratch his foot, pulled a swatch of the plant from under the front seat.

"O Jesus!" moaned my father. "It's Spanish moss. The goddam stuff is full of chiggers."

"Calvin! Don't talk like that."

"How the hell did it get in the car?"

"There's more," said my brother and he pulled up another handful. And another.

"It's behind the seat, too," my sister said.

"It's everywhere! The car is full of it!"

My father pulled off the road and soon we were standing around the car, scratching and pulling the Spanish moss out as fast as we could.

"Who did it?" my father roared.

But of course he and everyone else knew who had done it.

"Why?" he asked me, his voice expressing genuine bewilderment. "What the hell were you thinking about?"

The question, like life itself, had no answer. All I could do was say that I didn't know it had red bugs in it.

"Have we gotten it all?"

"Yeah. That's it."

But it wasn't. There was still the clump in my pocket. It would remain there, chiggers or not, all the way to Atlanta.

"What are we going to do?" my sister asked. Her legs were covered with red splotches.

"We need clear fingernail polish," my mother said. "If you cover the bites with it, it kills the chiggers. It's the only cure."

"Goddam it, we'll need about a gallon."

We stopped in the next town — Unadilla, I think — and bought the fingernail polish. By the time we reached Atlanta, long hours later, we were covered with sores that glistened with their coating of lacquer. And we were still scratching, as we would be for days.

After everyone was asleep, I got out of bed, pulled on my blue jeans and slipped out of the house. Once again, a half moon hung low in the sky, but now it illuminated the silent solid houses that stretched all around me, their low slung serenity broken only by the steeple of the Baptist church a block away. The only sounds were the occasional whine of an automobile and, far away, the wail of a train whistle. But when I reached in my pocket and touched the Spanish moss, I could hear the sound of the sea pounding on the beach. For a moment I stood alone between the ocean and the stars. Then I took my talisman from my pocket and draped it from the lower branch of the dogwood tree that stood in the front yard.

"What are you doing?"

I turned. My father was a dark shape standing on the porch.

"Nothing."

"You better come in the house. You shouldn't be out there."

"I don't want to. I want to stay out here."

He leaned forward and the moonlight caught his face. He started to say something, just as he had started to say something that afternoon at the beach. His lips even began to move. And then he stopped, abandoned whatever stern command his lips were forming. For a long time he stared at me.

"All right," he said. "Do as you please."

His face hung for a moment in moonlight — wistful, at once joyous and sad — before it fell back into the darkness. But his words lingered in the air and it wasn't the Spanish moss or the taste of papaya juice or the sea or that shadowy companion that would haunt me down the years, but his words, solid and ephemeral as the sound of waves breaking on the sand.

-2-

It was hard to go back to delivering papers. It wasn't the sort of thing the people in the circle that I wanted to be a part of—the athletes—did. It was the sort of thing, I discovered to my dismay, that Clark, a short squat four-eyed nonentity did. We crossed paths from time to time, loaded down with papers, but mercifully he seemed no more interested in associating with me than I was in associating with him. But even worse was the fact that the paper route limited my time with Vicki, time that was very limited to begin with. Because she was a Catholic and attended the girls' convent school, I saw her only in the afternoon and in the spring and summer after dinner when the children in the neighborhood played until dark. And often when I did see her, she was with her friend Marilyn, a short mousy girl whom I saw from time to time because she went to my school and who, as far as I could tell, never said anything, either at school or when I was with Vicki—a silent irritating presence.

But one afternoon I managed to find Vicki alone and I smuggled my curious object and my microscope out of the house and let her examine it in a nearby vacant lot.

"It's just a rock," she said.

I smiled knowingly.

"That's all it is," she insisted. "I know. We've been studying rocks in science."

I kept on smiling. What else would they tell her in a girls' school? And a Catholic school, too. She became furious and called me "silly" and "an idiot," but nothing could change the fact that she was not allowed to wear makeup or go out with boys (she even had to sneak off to the vacant lot) while the girls her age in the public school were already dating in cars. I wasn't above taking advantage of her humiliation and naiveté.

"I bet Virginia knows what it is," I said. Virginia, who lived next door to Vicki, was always going out with boys, even though she was Vicki's age—two months younger, in fact.

Virginia was part of the other mystery, Virginia and Vicki's brother Johnny, who was seventeen and wild. While the other boys broke street lamps with rocks and air rifles, Johnny did it with a .22 rifle—his own rifle, given to him on his birthday by his father. Like the other boys, I admired and feared him. I found his wildness romantic.

"That boy's crazy," my mother said. "Don't his parents know that? And then to turn around and give him a gun."

Crazy. What did the word apply to? The way he drove his father's car at breakneck speed up and down the quiet neighborhood streets? The way he treated Virginia, tossing her about, mussing her hair, teasing her with words I only vaguely understood? Or did *crazy* have something to do with what I saw at the lake?

One quiet afternoon I was fishing when I heard the murmur of voices in the small patch of woods between the two creeks that fed the lake. I feared, as I crept toward the voices, that the sound of the grasshoppers leaping away from my feet would give me away, it was so quiet. But as I came closer the tone of the voices—the urgency of the pleading, the confusion and uncertainty of protests broken by heavy breathing—told me that I needn't fear being noticed. And then I saw Johnny and Virginia lying in the high grass.

Somehow it didn't fit. What I read about my object—a book checked out of the Buckhead branch of the

Carnegie library — was full of facts pertaining to the importance of it: it had always to exist within a certain range of temperature; one hung slightly lower than the other lest they crush each other when a man sat down; it was essential to "procreation," which seemed to mean that without it — or them — one could not have babies or rather cause a woman to have babies. What did all that have to do with what I had seen in the high grass? I read another book, *Biology for Christians,* in which the author devoted little space to it except to say that the perfect design and function of it was further proof of the existence of God. That had an authoritative ring since my English teacher had told me that one could find God in a grain of sand. But as I held it in my hand and rolled it on my fingertips I wondered how God and what I had seen in the high grass could both be bound up with the hard rough object.

"It's just not healthy," Virginia's mother, Mrs. Simpkins, said to my mother. They had come together at the fence and each stood with a trowel in her hand, talking. Around them the earth they had been turning was damp and glistened in the sun. "Sticking a girl off in a convent that way."

My mother nodded gravely.

"I mean, coeducation is best."

"Lord knows, he doesn't hide his son away."

Mrs. Simpkins leaned forward. "Oh, *he* can explain that." The he, I knew, was Mr. Maloney, a somewhat notorious character in the neighborhood. "He says, 'Girls are helpless. You have to protect them. But you just give boys their head and let them go.' Now I ask you!"

"They're Catholic."

Mrs. Simpkins nodded. "Put them all together, I say. Do away with the double standard and you know what you'll find? That girls are by nature pure. It's hiding them away that turns them bad."

Double standard. I was vaguely familiar with the term, my mother having hurled it at my father once or twice. Still, I wasn't sure what it meant, though most certainly poor Vicki was a victim of it. I resolved to be nicer to her but found it difficult since she was so ruled by the double standard. Her mother didn't seem to worry much, the reason being, as I overheard her say to her husband one day, "He's so young. There's no danger in their seeing each other." And the father even relented a little so that I could walk with her to the drugstore or sit in the front yard and talk to her.

But there were limits. Once we wandered off to the lake together and were sitting by the water when a car roared to a stop and Mr. Maloney leaped out. As he rushed toward us I considered diving into the water to escape, but my fear of the murky depths balanced my fear of the man. Mr. Maloney grabbed Vicki by the arm and glared at me for a moment before he dragged her away to the car. The glare was filled with something that froze my blood — the opposite of what I had felt on seeing Virginia and Johnny in the high grass when my blood roared wildly and caused my heart to pound. Suppose Mr. Maloney ever discovered that I had shown my object to Vicki, the same object so mysteriously bound up with his son Johnny and Virginia?

It was all very confusing, and on Sunday the preacher didn't help much. My mind was still filled with what I had heard that very morning, that Johnny had "finally got himself thrown in jail," as his father put it. Virginia, in a pink and white dress that she continually looked down at, sat across from me on the other side of the balcony and Dr. Wiley said, "The skeptic cannot deny that there are things we all are certain of. In philosophy this feeling is called 'spontaneous certitude.' What are these things? Love, devotion, honor, duty. And, yes, hate, envy, lust, greed." *Spontaneous certitude*. Things we know automatically, without thinking. But what if these things contradict each other?

After church as I walked down the Baptist side of the road (because the Baptist church was on that side, the Catholic on the other), I looked across and saw on the Catholic side Mr. and Mrs. Maloney and Vicki with a scarf over her head, her eyes fixed on her feet, and behind them Johnny, large, expansive, grinning, waving to people on both sides of the road. In jail last night, obviously bailed out by his father, now coming from church. It struck me that Johnny's life must be one spontaneous certitude after another, and I found myself longing for one — just one — a longing somehow bound up with the way I couldn't take my eyes off the obviously embarrassed Vicki, though I couldn't comprehend what the connection was.

But whatever it was, it grew stronger. During the hot, molasses-like summer afternoons, I sat with her in her backyard. Her father was at work and her mother was often at the church doing committee and social work. Johnny appeared sporadically, always loud and moving rapidly about, occasionally opening and gulping down bottles of beer. Of course, I wasn't supposed to be there, but we knew Johnny wouldn't tell and even Mrs. Maloney, when she found us, didn't seem concerned. Only when Mr. Maloney, who was a salesman of some kind, came home unexpectedly, did I have to scramble for the bushes at the back of the yard and sneak away.

I sensed that Vicki allowed me to come only because she was trapped, isolated. I was a living being, someone to talk to, to listen to, a relief from book after book, from watching the birds and occasionally working in the flower beds. She patronized me unmercifully with her superior knowledge, exerting her age and maturity, but I knew that I admired not so much what she said as the way she turned her head, the slender lines of her neck, her long legs. I also saw how in the midst of her youthful pedantry and condescension she became suddenly confused and bewildered by my eyes, and since I was at those moments confused and bewildered myself, we often lapsed into a mutual sensual dalliance: she so totally ignorant of physical realities; I stirred by feelings I understood only from the words of others, from what I had seen that afternoon in the high grass, from what I had read about my mysterious object. It was only natural, desperate as I was by the time July was plodding to its end, that I seize upon my only advantage, and one afternoon I took my object and microscope and went to see her. But Johnny was there.

"Don't you two ever go anywhere?" he asked.

"I can't," his sister said. "You know that."

"Oh, Dad won't be home for hours and Mom's at church. Here."

He reached in his pocket and took out some coins. "Go to a movie. There's a good one playing at the Buckhead."

Vicki leapt at the opportunity but at the same time despaired of having the daring to take advantage of it. "I can't leave the house."

"Sure you can. Go on. Both of you. Look, it starts at two thirty. It's one now."

She looked eagerly at me, and I couldn't deny her. I nodded.

"All right," she said. "We will."

"Good!" He gave her the money.

She wanted to leave right away but I pointed out that it would take only fifteen minutes to get there, so we had an hour and fifteen minutes to kill.

"Of course," she said, "you probably won't understand the movie."

"I will too."

"No, you're too young."

"I know more than you do."

She tossed her head back and laughed. She was not being purposefully malicious; she was merely excited and happy. Yet her indifference to all save her own excitement aroused something in me and with mixed feelings and pounding heart, I fired back at her, "Then I suppose you know what this is." I opened my hand and revealed my prize.

"Oh, that rock."

"It's not a rock."

"Yes, it *is.* I'm tired of that game."

"No, it isn't. It's . . . it's a testicle."

"A what?" All the excitement in her eyes changed instantly to uncertainty.

What followed was a long, awkward description of what I called sexual intercourse, a description which grew naturally from my attempt to explain the function and purpose of my object. Vicki gulped, nodded her head from time to time and listened. The tables were turned, I was patronizing her, but my delight was tempered by stirrings within myself, for I felt that my little lecture was simply words skimming on the surface of something deep and unfathomable. I hesitated. I trembled. "Let's go in the house where we can see it through the microscope," I said.

She hesitated. "The movie," she said softly.

"We have lots of time." Actually it was already past time.

"All right." She turned and I followed her into the kitchen, where she stopped.

"We can use the table in here." The shining white walls, the immaculate cabinets, the glistening sink and spotless glaring tile floor, the gas range with its burners, the refrigerator—the surroundings were hopelessly inappropriate but I could think of no convincing argument against her suggestion. In fact, I could think of nothing, not even what I would do—or was supposed to do—at the next moment. I put the microscope on the table and we both peered through it and discussed the outrageous capability of such an ordinary object. She picked it up and held it out in her open hand; I reached for it and our hands met and closed around it.

The front door slammed shut.

Our hands tightened together so that I felt the object pressing into my palm. We're caught, we both seemed to say, so what's the use? Then we heard Johnny's loud voice, Virginia's high-pitched giggles. We heard them move through the living room and up the stairs—to the bedrooms. The loud talk, the giggling gave way to a deep silence broken occasionally by a barely audible whisper, a low laugh, mysterious thumps on the floor, the unmistakable sounds of movement on a bed.

I saw Vicki's eyes narrow and harden and I didn't know how to interpret the effect the intrusion had had upon her, but I feared the worst. Yet even as I despaired (of what? I still didn't know) I felt Vicki's hand drawing me toward her. After that the glare of the kitchen became a swirl of light, the sharp clean surfaces hazards as we moved awkwardly against one another, depending upon spontaneous certitude (the phrase ran idiotically through my reeling brain) to guide them. The precious object fell to the floor and rolled bumpily several inches — the sound of it an echoing thump and roar. I was dimly aware of noises overhead, shouts, laughter, the sound of running feet. But only dimly. We fumbled with one another, amazed that failed experiments didn't deter the wild desire that drove us on. The tile was cold against my body. Her blouse was undone, her skirt half off, my pants caught by a physical phenomenon I struggled to overcome. I knew what to do, I had told her what was done — we were trying desperately to work out the how (I saw the ridiculous distorted reflection of our two half-naked bodies in the sparkling surface of the oven door) when a loud explosion filled the air.

Her father has come home and shot me, I thought, and in my mind's eye I saw the man standing in the kitchen door, a gun smoking in his hand. We rolled apart. There was no one in the doorway. We waited. A scream echoed through the house, followed by another and another. We sat up but remained next to one another, our legs spread in front of us, our hands on the floor behind our backs, our shoulders touching, and we stared first up at the ceiling and then at each other. We heard noise on the stairs, the sound of a table turning over in the living room, and then the doorway was filled with Johnny, clutching his left shoulder with his right hand, his face dazed, bewildered, the left side of his body covered in blood. Overhead, Virginia was screaming again.

Vicki recovered first. As she started for the telephone to call the hospital she shouted back to me, "Get Virginia out! And get yourself out! Quick!", perhaps sensing in her new awareness of reality that what the neighbors, who were sure to come streaming in, were about to discover would look very much like an orgy. I was up the stairs in a flash, even though I dressed as I ran, and I found a pitiful naked Virginia sitting on the bed, Johnny's .22 rifle lying at her feet. She seemed not to see me, so hysterical she was. She screamed and screamed and screamed and I said, "To hell with it" (my first natural, unselfconscious use of swearing) and flew back down to the kitchen, past the groaning Johnny. One thing was sure—I was going to get out; the picture of Vicki's father with the gun was still quite vivid in my mind. As I crossed the kitchen, snatching up the microscope as I went, my bare foot was painfully stung by something. I looked down and saw that I had stepped on my object, but what I really noticed was that I had no shoes on. I found one by the refrigerator, the other by the sink, and holding them in one hand, the microscope in the other, I ran out the back door, scrambled over the chainlink fence and into the bushes. Virginia was still screaming, and all up and down the street I heard the noise of screen doors slamming shut.

Only after a large crowd had gathered around the house and Mr. Maloney had gotten home and Virginia's mother had discovered her screaming naked daughter and the wail of the ambulance coming from town filled the air—only then did I creep up to the edge of the crowd. Virginia's mother and Mr. Maloney had confronted one another on the raised front porch and their words and actions became a scene played out on a stage for the fascinated audience on the front lawn.

". . . ought to be in jail!" the woman screamed. "Or in an insane asylum!"

"She came here!" he shouted back. "She was in my house! If you looked after her, this wouldn't have happened. You don't see Vicki . . ."

"Oh, yes, keep her locked up. Like you do. No, I trust

my neighbors and friends. Or I used to. Let me tell you something, you haven't heard the last of this."

"Probably not, if you let her keep running around."

"You son-of-a-bitch!" She swung at him but he caught her arm.

"She's underage! She's only sixteen. I'll have him up for . . ."

"For rape?" Mr. Maloney roared with laughter. "Then I'll have her up for attempted murder."

"She was defending herself."

He laughed again. "Five minutes ago you said he shot himself. That it was an accident."

By now two neighbors had put their arms around the woman and were drawing her away. "I'll get you!" she shouted. "I swear I will!"

"The trouble is," a woman near me whispered as Mrs. Simpkins was led through the crowd, "they don't teach sex education in the schools."

The ambulance arrived. Two aides carried a stretcher into the house and a few moments later they came out, half-rolling, half-carrying a somewhat somber Johnny.

"It's not serious," someone said.

"Only the shoulder. He'll be all right."

The police arrived and told everyone that it was "all over" and to go home. Gradually the crowd broke up and very few remained when Vicki came out on the porch. She caught my eye and motioned me around to the backyard. She went through the house and met me there. "You've got to say you were here," she said, her voice full of dread.

"But . . . why?"

"I don't know. It's the police. They . . . they claim they have to have proof that Johnny didn't . . . make her come in."

"But you were here."

"No, I'm his sister. They say . . ."

"You told them."

"Only that you were here playing."

"But your father."

She looked down.

Filled with fear that bordered on panic — stunned, in fact — I followed her toward the kitchen, but before I was well into the room Mr. Maloney shouted, "Were you here when all this happened?"

He was standing next to the table and off to one side were the two policemen. Recovering from the initial onslaught, I said (so loudly I surprised myself), "Yes."

Mr. Maloney's face went blood-red but I, who in the last hour had learned more about reading faces than I had in all the previous years of my life, saw in the eyes the glare of the trapped animal, uncertain as to what to do, how to escape.

"We'll do the questioning," said one of the policemen, his voice full of weariness. "Were you here when Mr. Maloney's son came in with the girl?"

"Yes."

"Did he force her into the house?"

"Well, I didn't see them. Vicki and I were here in the kitchen looking at . . . something through a microscope. But I heard them. She was laughing and he was joking and . . . no, he didn't force her in."

"All right," the policeman said, his tone reflecting that I had simply confirmed what he already knew. "I don't suppose you saw the shooting."

"No. I only heard it."

He nodded. "Okay. That's all."

"Why did you run, you little bastard?" Mr. Maloney hissed.

"What?"

"Why did you run if you were only looking through a microscope?"

"I was afraid. I mean, the gunshot and all."

"You lying son-of-a-bitch. I ought to kill you."

I had turned my eyes from the man to the floor, and Mr. Maloney probably thought I was afraid; but soon he realized that I was simply looking around.

"What is it?" asked the policeman. "I said you could go."

"My rock. I'm looking for my rock."

Mr. Maloney exploded and lunged toward me, but the policemen grabbed him and held him back. "Get on out, son," one of them said.

I went out through the back door and paused in the yard for a moment to look around, but I saw no one. The neighborhood had returned to its summer silence. I walked around the house and as I was passing the side of it I heard my name. I looked up and saw Vicki at the window.

"Here," she whispered, and she tossed me my object. I caught it.

"You'll come back, won't you?"

"Vicki!" her father shouted from the kitchen. She pulled her head in and disappeared.

The neighborhood had settled back into its customary silence. The afternoon sun beat down unmercifully on the trees, the flowers, the grass, the imperturbable houses, everything that made up the world as I had always known it.

You'll come back, won't you.

I stood for a long time by the side of the house before I hurled the object high in the air and watched it arch gracefully into the bushes at the far side of the next yard. I would never be able to find it but that didn't matter. I knew with spontaneous certitude that I didn't need it anymore.

-*3*-

Toward the end of that summer Allen came back, reappeared. I couldn't figure out why and I asked my mother but all she said was that he was probably lonely.

And Allen didn't talk much. Mostly we played basketball on the outdoor court. Afterwards, seared by the heat, our eyes so full of sweat we could hardly see, we walked to Garden Hills where I bought a Coca-Cola in the drugstore while Allen went into Sam's Bar for a beer. I was too young to go into Sam's. I stood on the sidewalk and tried to see him through the glass front. Sometimes he lingered for a moment, leaned on the bar and became one of the shapes, his head moving slightly as he talked. But all I could hear was a low murmur.

After he came out with his bottle of beer, we walked to the stream that ran through the small park three blocks away where Allen took off his shoes and socks and lay down, his body stretching from the stream almost to the top of the bank. He lay on his side, one arm thrown over his head to shield his eyes from the sun, his long legs wrapped around each other like two snakes down to his bare feet. And then we talked. Or rather, I talked. Allen seldom said anything, he just listened to me ramble on. I don't remember much about those "conversations"; I mean, I don't remember many of the words. I can see him sprawled on the bank. I can see myself sitting on the other side of the little stream, staring at him. And I can see the stream, the slow-moving brown water, and all around it the weeds and honeysuckle vines and privet. And I remember that I felt, there beside the stream, what I had felt when I looked into the bar — a sense of something alien, something not at ease in the heat of those suburban afternoons. It was probably that something—whatever it was—that caused the one conversation I do remember.

"I'm going to leave home as soon as I can," I said.

"Oh. Where will you go?"

Even that was different. He was a grown man, an adult, but he hadn't protested, hadn't told me to "get an education." Yet how could I answer his question? All I had were daydreams in which I saw myself in strange cities, in enormous flat fields, in the desert, in mountains, always moving, alone except for those mysterious women who had begun to haunt me at the beach.

"I don't know. Anywhere . . . places you went. You know."

He said, seemingly talking to the ground that he was staring at, "Why not? Just get the hell out of here. Let me tell you, it's great. I mean, to be away from everything, from everybody."

"You think so?"

"Sure."

"Then why did you come back?"

He laughed. "I haven't come back. Not the way you mean. That's what they all think, but let me tell you, if you leave, then . . . then you don't have to worry . . ." He trailed off and took a drink from his bottle. "The best place to go is New Orleans. In New Orleans you can get anything you want—you can do anything you want." His body went rigid, the veins in his skinny neck bulged and his hand tightened around the bottle until the skin over the knuckles went white. "Go to New Orleans first," he half shouted, "and you won't have to go anywhere else." He hurled the bottle. It tumbled through the air and shattered against the rocks far down the stream. Then his body relaxed and we both stared for a moment at the shattered glass sparkling in a shaft of sunlight.

"Come on," he said, "I have to get . . . to get back to the house."

Allen was a confusing presence. I saw him only in the daytime, yet he was a part of my night world, the world of Minnie and Mary, of my father's face in the moonlight, though at the time I couldn't go back, couldn't make connections. There was something malignant about him, the malignancy of freedom that in the warm security of the bright summer neighborhood made him seem a menace, threatening. But at night the thought of him came to me like an angel. And on those Sunday mornings before dawn he was with me as I pedaled in the dark. But not real, not solid. He couldn't move bodily from my day world to my night one. I could still believe in the separation between night and day, between past and present, because I still didn't understand the power of *things*, of ceiling fans and tile floors, of brick and wood, of odd-shaped bottles and cold hard cylinders packed with ice cream.

And a shoe box.

The one that had always been in grandmother's room, that she let me go through from time to time. The kind of box in which you always find something "new," and buried in a stack of old photographs and invitations and postcards with pictures of The Moon Over Miami and My Old Kentucky Home I came upon a photograph of a man hanging by his neck from a tree. "Who is he?" I asked.

"That's the Jew who killed poor Mary Phagan," my grandmother said.

"And they hanged him for it?"

"Well, the state was supposed to. But Governor Slaton commuted the sentence to life in prison and a lynch mob went to Milledgeville and got him and brought him back to Marietta and hanged him. They almost got Governor

Slaton, too. A mob went out to his house but the police kept them out. It was the last thing he did as governor. After that he had to leave the country for awhile."

"You mean his house in Buckhead?"

"Yes."

I had heard of Leo Frank but now he was an object, solid in my hand: the rope tight around his neck, his shirt untucked, barefoot (Why is he barefoot? I remember wondering). And he smelled of my grandmother's lilac powder, which placed him in time more concretely even than the clothes on the men, women and children who stared up at him, a dead man hanging from a tree. Only after I had seen that photograph, which had frozen for all time the fleshy manifestation of hate, captured a violence that touched something deep within me—only then did the photographs of my relatives, grandparents and aunts and uncles, begin to come to life; only then did the faces beneath the ridiculous hairstyles and the hands folded stiffly in the laps begin to move. And only after that could I imagine the mob that moved up Peachtree Road, slogging through mud from what was then the end of the tram line at Peachtree Creek. Not in the distant past but in 1915 when my father, ten years old at the time—not much younger than myself—looked into the angry faces of the men.

Now I sensed the presence of something alien in the streets I roamed; I realized that the Yankee Italian liquor store owner had come from somewhere else, that Abraham may have stood on the sidewalk in front of his shop and watched the mob charge the fence around the Slaton estate, that the old druggist was haunted by a fear of poverty that existed somewhere outside the Buckhead I lived in. Like the black men, they came from and went to places I knew nothing about. But it was more than that;

they were alien — but they had come to Garden Hills
before me, before I was born. And that meant that there
was some sense in which *I* was alien, a part of someone
else's world as I pedaled through the dark. Gradually in
the full light of day I began to feel those dark buildings,
heard the howl of the dogs, and, when I rode through
Garden Hills and looked into the glass storefronts, I
began to see myself, a ghost on a bicycle sneaking glances
at the great estate across the street. That image recurred,
day after day, week after week, and I think it was to escape it that, after the papers were delivered on Sunday
morning but while it was still dark, I started going to
Hawley's Fruit Stand.

Unlike almost everyone else in Garden Hills and Buckhead Hawley opened on Sunday. What's more, he opened
or at least got to his store before dawn to arrange and
display the produce that he had hauled from the farmers'
market on the other side of the city or that local farmers
had left on the sidewalk in front of his store. His shop
glowed in the dark with a dim warm light that fell in a
rectangle across the sidewalk and into the road: a beacon
shining directly across the street from the Slaton estate.
And then, while I was still far away, I smelled it: a medley
of odors — potatoes and tomatoes and beans and corn
mixed with the pungent aroma of citrus fruit — that grew
stronger and stronger until finally, just before I got off my
bicycle and kicked down its stand, I caught the sweet
scent of flowers. A haven, an outpost of nature. Maybe a
reminder of my own middle Georgia background, that
farm that my grandmother and her brothers and sisters
were raised on. But it wasn't the smells that drew me to
it. No, I dodged the baskets of flowers hanging from the
awning that stretched over the sidewalk and squeezed
through tight rows of fruit and vegetable bins to get to

the small room in the back, a dingy room illuminated by one naked lightbulb hanging from a cord, a room that had replaced my basement room as a place of refuge. But rather than books, it contained a pinball machine.

It was a truly wonderful creation that made strange bell-like noises and was filled with lights that flashed orange, red, yellow and purple. I pumped most of my meager earnings into that machine, stood there amid the smells of watermelons and peaches and oranges, a Nehi Grape bottle making a circle on the glass above the flashing lights and, lost in a battle against the silver ball that darted about the board so rapidly and erratically that only the quickest reflexes could move the flippers at just the right time, I forgot the two worlds outside the door, one fading now into the other as night gave way to day. For an hour or so I fell into the machine and wandered in its labyrinth.

When my money ran out or when I realized that I had to get home to eat breakfast and get to Sunday school and I pulled away from the pinball machine—maze within maze—and weaved through the bins and hanging baskets and finally out onto the street, the Slaton estate was still there, seemingly harmless in the bright morning sunlight, but I knew the truth about it—and about Garden Hills. Exactly what that truth was I couldn't say, but I could manage the breakup of the world around me, its sudden fluidity, so long as *I* remained the same, constant, unchanging, somehow detached from both worlds. And so long as—at the terrible hour of dawn when the first rays of sunlight struck the tops of the buildings and the connection between the two worlds became palpable as darkness faded into, became a part of, daylight—I could escape into the back room and lose myself in the pinball machine.

But it couldn't last. One day as I was riding through Garden Hills, I turned my head and saw my reflection in the glass storefronts. But it wasn't myself, pedaling in the sunlight. It was that other *self*, my ghost, pedaling in the dark. I looked away and looked back and my ghost was gone; I was I, riding in the light. During the weeks that followed, that image came and went until I grew used to it, accepted it as an uncontrollable act of my imagination. And then one day, one of those late August days when the sky is a blinding glare from horizon to horizon, I turned my head and saw my ghost. As usual, I looked ahead and then looked back. My ghost was still there. I blinked my eyes but still my other self didn't go away. And then, suddenly, he did go away and I saw myself in the daylight, an accurate reflection, it seemed, until I looked ahead once again and . . . it was dark and the Slaton estate loomed ominously on my left and I heard the howl of the dogs and I turned my head and in the dim glass of the storefronts, there I was, a reflection in the window, pedaling furiously and happily in the sunlight.

What had happened? I looked up at the sky; it was first dark, filled with stars, then so bright I couldn't find the sun in the glare. For a moment—maybe longer than a moment—time seemed to cease. I was everywhere and nowhere.

A severe jolt shook my body; the handlebars jammed against my hand and the front wheel turned first one way, then the other. Someone shouted, "Look out, son!" And then I was riding in the gutter. Speeding cars missed me by inches; people blew their horns. Finally, at a driveway I turned the bicycle back onto the sidewalk and came to a stop.

The man who had shouted at me when I hit the curb, over a block away now, shook his head, turned and went on his way. I was standing astraddle my bicycle in the middle of the sidewalk between Garden Hills and Buckhead on a hot summer day. Maybe I had almost been killed; it didn't matter. What did matter was that the day remain the day, the place the place. Days and weeks would pass. And then years. Whether or not it would ever happen again didn't matter either because at any moment it *could* happen. And the further I lived away from that day, the more it seemed that everything—the paper route, the estate, the dogs, the shoe box—had been leading up to that instant when, having realized that I was an alien in the neighborhood I had grown up in, I finally pedaled right out of myself.

And strange to say, the Sunday morning that followed that mysterious moment seemed not quite as frightening, maybe because I had learned that escaping could be even more terrifying. Almost automatically, when the last paper was delivered, I went to Hawley's, pushed my way through to the back room, pumped my nickel in the machine and felt something of the old thrill when the bells rang, the lights flashed and the ball slammed into the slot with a bang.

But it wasn't the same. It was a game. A game I enjoyed immensely but I couldn't lose myself in it, couldn't lose the sense of myself playing a game. No matter how skillful I was, no matter how long I kept the ball in motion, inevitably it slipped through, fell into the hole and disappeared. The pinball machine was a deception, a false turn, a blind alley, the first of countless "escapes" I would try until I learned from failure, realized that any escape that doesn't acknowledge a reality that is inescapable is a game.

-*4*-

She was standing at the window, one hand resting on the sill beneath her breasts, the other fiddling with the venetian blind cord. It was, I soon learned, her favorite place. She stared out at the covered passageway that ran from the annex to the old building and occasionally her eyes drifted over to the new gym or maybe to the football field that stretched out behind it. Sometimes sunlight broke over her blouse, sometimes rain streaked the glass, and the wood that separated the panes formed bars between her and whatever she was staring at.

Miss Wagner taught English and Latin and what she taught was important because she was still young (though of course I didn't realize that at the time), and she couldn't really distinguish what we could understand from what we couldn't. In a math or a science teacher such a lack of discernment leads to disaster but in literature it can be a great advantage if it's coupled with enthusiasm. I still have Miss Wagner's copy of Norton's translation of the *Divine Comedy*, the first of numerous books I was to "borrow" from teachers and friends over the years, and whenever my eye falls on it in the bookshelf, I remember the anxious expression on her face as she placed the book in my hands and said, "You can't understand anything about civilization, about culture, if you haven't read Dante."

I tried, but I couldn't read Dante. I was too young. Yet the conviction — her conviction — that I should read Dante stayed with me until, years later, I *did* read him, although by then it was too late.

Her convictions became the convictions of her students. This happened not only because she was

119

enthusiastic—students are quick to detect empty enthusiasm. She delighted in us, laughed with and at us, and she
knew what so few teachers of adolescents seem to know,
that teenagers sense instinctively the unbreakable link
between style and substance, between word and deed. So
when I wrote a silly little poem that contained the refrain,
"Give me a girl in my arms and a beer in my hand/And
the rest of the world be damned," and it was passed
around among giggling students until she confiscated and
read it, she didn't keep me after school or send me to the
principal or write a note to my parents. She didn't even
give me a lecture. Instead, she read the poem aloud to
the class, analyzed it and determined that it was—in
form, meter and rhythm—a second-rate imitation of "The
House by the Side of the Road," a decidedly second-rate
poem. Her eyes burned into me as she said, "What's
wrong with your poem is that it's *insincere*."

She knew and I knew that I had never really had a girl
in my arms or a beer in my hand and I certainly didn't
know what "the rest of the world" was, let alone whether
or not it should "be damned."

"In other words, it has no *style*," she said. "It's insincere because *you* are insincere."

I knew that she had gone beyond the poem to something else, but how could I distinguish between style and
insincerity, lost as I was in a world in which girls (well,
Vicki) said one thing and did another, in which miserly
druggists weighed quarts of ice cream, in which packs of
vicious dogs protected ex-politicians, in which wives and
husbands danced a dance of duty and deception. I walked
out of Miss Wagner's English class, my head full of lofty
pronouncements I only half understood, my ears ringing
with poetry, and onto . . . the football field for drill.

Because two years of R.O.T.C. were required of every high school boy. We were issued uniforms (thick wool, totally inappropriate for all but two months of the year) and M-1 rifles, minus firing pins. We saw movies about venereal disease and how to dress a wound ("Remember, the hole where the bullet comes out is always larger than the one where it went in"), listened to two sergeants tell combat stories, and, to prepare us for the years ahead, learned to field strip an M-1 rifle. (It's interesting to contemplate the fact that practically every middle-aged American man can field strip an M-1 rifle.) And twice a week we drilled in uniform on the football field. The officers (juniors and seniors who had volunteered past the required two years) wore Sam Brown belts and swords and shouted the commands, and the rest of us in our hot, bulky, ill-fitting uniforms executed right and left turns and flanking movements, performed "To the rear, march!" over and over again, and mutilated our thumbs during inspection of arms. I never doubted that what we were doing was important, but I could never figure out what it had to do with the exploits I saw John Wayne perform at the movies on Saturday. Ludicrous as the ill-fitting uniforms and impotent rifles were, I—and I suspect all of us—managed to maintain our fantasies of women melting into the arms of heroes. And the sergeants told us that it all had to do with "teamwork," that drilling taught us to act in unison and to trust our "buddies," advice not unlike that given us by football and basketball coaches. All of which was fine and good unless your "buddy" happened to be Clark. One thing seemed certain to us: Clark would never know the thrill of victory in combat or with women.

Not that we didn't like him; we just couldn't figure him out. He was short and stocky and talked like a hick but he also had a terrible case of acne and wore thick glasses. He seemed a cross between a redneck and a bookworm, an impossible combination. Exactly what he was, I never figured out; whatever he was, he turned the drill field into a disaster area.

On the first few drill days his "problem" didn't show up, and before I learned the truth I often wondered why. The only answer I could think of was that for a while he was lucky. At each command of "column right" or "column left" he guessed correctly (he did have a fifty-fifty chance, of course, and there were times, as when we were marching by the stadium seats, that a turn in only one direction was possible). But as I was learning in math, odds even out as numbers increase and by our third or fourth drilling session Clark's problem became apparent; we could no longer put down his mistakes to a lack of concentration. Quite simply, he didn't know his right from his left.

Now Clark wasn't retarded or a spastic (we had several of both in school); we thought he was just plain stupid (that he was unfailingly pleasant and smiled constantly through his thick glasses merely reinforced this opinion); doubtless his parents thought him "absentminded." I don't know what the teachers thought of him, but I certainly found out what Sergeant Masters thought of him.

Clark's place was next to my own so when we were marching he was directly ahead of me in line; consequently, I bore the brunt of his incompetence. I was run into from the rear; rifle sights were driven into my forehead; falling bodies crashed into my own. In fact, those of us around Clark were knocked about far more than he was. "Column right, march!" the lieutenant would shout and to the left Clark would go, crashing head-on into the person next to him, who tumbled diagonally into me, who fell sideways against the trooper in the next column. And Clark stood serenely in the middle of the chaos, smiling through his thick glasses.

At first we thought it very funny, and for awhile after that we didn't mind it because it broke up the monotony of drilling: every simple maneuver was an adventure if you had Clark in your platoon, and since our lieutenant was particularly obnoxious, we enjoyed seeing his authority unwittingly broken by a clod like Clark. But finally it got to us, too, and we began to kick and poke him and curse him when he made a mistake. Our abuse didn't seem to bother him; he took whatever we had to offer and kept on smiling. We had to face the truth: Clark didn't know his right from his left because he was an idiot.

Several of us knew that Sergeant Masters had noticed and we wondered why he didn't intervene. Of course, he had problems of his own. He had recently gotten into a fight in the middle of the schoolyard and Coach Murphy, an ex-tackle at the University of Georgia, had flattened him. News of the fight and of what started it — Coach Murphy referred to one of the teachers as a "whore" — spread through the school like wildfire. We were used to fights between students, but a fight between two teachers was something new, different. And which teacher had Coach Murphy called a whore? Was it even really a teacher he had been referring to? The main candidate was Miss Greybill, the new, young English and drama teacher.

A group — Miss Wagner's "protegees" — gathered around her desk after class and tried to get the whole story out of her. "What caused it?" someone asked.

"Were they really fighting over a woman?"

She brushed our questions aside. "It's simple," she said. "Coach Murphy is a bully."

"But Sergeant Masters must have done something. Or said something."

"No. Sergeant Masters didn't do or say anything. Coach Murphy is a bully. *All* football players are bullies."

Heads nodded. All but my own. I hovered at the back, neither a part of the group nor separate from it. I was a football player, or rather I wanted very much to be one, to make the team. But I also wanted to learn Latin and read books. The problem was, the people who did those things, the people gathered around Miss Wagner weren't . . . weren't my kind of people. The boys hadn't developed the slouch of the athlete and seemed effeminate, something like Europeans in foreign movies. And the girls may or may not have been pretty; you couldn't tell because they didn't seem to be able to get their clothes right. Either they didn't have the right blouses and skirts and thin white socks and black ballerina slippers or else they somehow didn't put them on right. They—the boys and the girls—were outsiders, not a part of the "popular" crowd and so to be pitied. Some, I discovered, were pitiful, but others were bitter and, most disturbing, some didn't seem to care at all, were cynical and satiric. But if I wanted to talk about books, I had to talk to them.

Because when I moved into that other circle—the athletes and cheerleaders and the hangers-on—I couldn't talk about books or classes or anything we were studying. The rule was that you never studied, which meant that you studied secretly. School—classes and books—were an aside, something you attended to in your spare time. What mattered were speed and clothes and guts and cars and dates, and above all what mattered was not seeming to care very much about any of these things. Take clothes. If you were a boy, you had to wear a white T-shirt and blue jeans and loafers. The clothes of someone who doesn't care about clothes and wants to make sure that everyone knows that he doesn't care about clothes. I admired these people,

I liked their "style," maybe because I mistook it for a genuine modesty, a refusal to show off—the true democratic spirit. Nothing is easier to rationalize than snobbery.

As we were leaving the room Miss Wagner called me back, and when all the others were gone, she said, "I meant that, you know."

"What?"

"That all football players are bullies."

I looked at her but didn't say anything.

"You're not going to argue?"

I shook my head.

"You have to decide, you know. You have to make up your mind. You can't go on much longer."

"What do you mean? What are you talking about?"

Her face grew very red and her voice erupted, "Get out! Damn it, get out!"

"But . . ."

"Get out!"

I didn't know why she had lost her temper, but I knew that I was shocked. It wasn't just that she cursed and I had never heard a teacher curse before. It wasn't that she knew I was playing dumb, pretending not to understand. Normally she would handle that the way she handled my poem. No, I felt that her anger was out of proportion to my . . . insincerity.

Sergeant Masters's black eye kept the fight alive for another day or two. Rumor had it that the two of them had been seen going into the principal's office soon after the event, just like two students. Gradually the affair faded as other events and rumors supplanted it. But nothing quite as spectacular as a fight between two teachers.

But probably Sergeant Masters, even though if you looked closely you could still see the black eye, was merely leaving the problem with Clark to Reynolds, giving him a chance to deal with it and solve it. Reynolds, I must admit, did his best. At first he cajoled and encouraged: "Come on, Thornwell, you can do better than that. Think! Concentrate!" He took him aside and gave him private lessons and ordered others to do the same. Ultimately he came to suspect that Clark was doing it on purpose. It was both delightful and pitiful to watch Clark gradually destroy him. Reynolds, who was what we would now call a born-again Christian, began by preaching to us, by trying to convince us that it was God's plan that we become good soldiers. Apropos of nothing whatsoever he would bring us to "at ease" and say things like: "Before you say anything about anybody else, ask yourself three questions: Is it true? It is necessary? Will it hurt anyone?" Naturally, after cajoling and encouragement and private lessons didn't help, Reynolds advised Clark to pray (quite literally) for guidance. Maybe Clark did pray — what his religion was was as unfathomable as everything else about him — but if he did, then God's answer must have been, "No."

It was at this point that Reynolds, apparently unable to accept the possibility that God would refuse a request, decided that Clark was doing it on purpose. His expression became a "knowing" one. "This won't get you out of R.O.T.C., you know," Reynolds said to him.

Clark stared out through his thick glasses. "I don't want to get out."

"Yeah, sure."

So time would solve the problem. Once Clark realized that he had to take R.O.T.C. no matter what, he would, as Reynolds put it, "Straighten up and fly right." But he didn't. He flew right and left indiscriminately week after week. And then, after all the other platoons were marching in a neat, orderly fashion up and down the football field and Sergeant Masters began commending their lieutenants for the fine job they were doing, the "truth" dawned on Reynolds and one day, after two or three of us had picked ourselves up off the ground and we were all standing at attention in ranks again, he said, "Okay, Thornwell, I know what you're up to."

Clark stared at him and said nothing.

"Well, it's not going to work. You want a battle? All right, I'll give you a battle. Every time you make a wrong turn, you do a lap. You understand?"

"Yes, Sir."

And so the laps began. 'Round and 'round the track went Clark. And every time he returned to the platoon, his marching was as erratic as ever. After that came pushups, which did nothing more than produce a red-faced panting Clark with steamed-up glasses who went left at the first command to go right. And finally, during a company parade before a visiting officer (a real one), Clark performed in such as manner as to make us what Sergeant Masters later called, "A disgrace to the United States Army." Reynolds's career was in jeopardy—he obviously had dreams of leading men in battle and a stumpy stubborn smartass was about to destroy that dream. The first drill day after the parade, Reynolds called Clark out of ranks and, facing him before the platoon, shouted in his face, "It's over, finished. You're gonna march right. You understand?"

Clark nodded his head, fell back into ranks and at the first command, "Column right!" turned smartly to the left.

"Halt!" screamed Reynolds, unnecessarily since Clark had once again singlehandedly brought the platoon to a standstill. "Halt, halt, halt!"

Reynolds charged into the ranks, parting the rest of us as he went, and when he got to Clark, he reached out and grabbed the knot of his tie. "You goddam son-of-a-bitch. I told you. Goddam it, I told you. I'll cut your balls off, you little bastard!"

Maybe that would have been the end of it. Maybe Reynolds would have realized that he was being ridiculous, that Christians don't talk that way, but at that moment someone, unable to resist the temptation, said, "Before you say anything about anybody else, ask yourself three questions," and Reynolds went berserk. He pulled his sword from its sheath and held the point against Clark's Adam's apple. Whether or not he would have slit his throat I don't know because at that moment Sergeant Masters, who must have heard the commotion, pushed his way through the ranks, placed his hand on Reynolds's wrist and slowly pushed the arm down until the sword pointed toward the ground. Obviously, Reynolds had not been able to solve the problem.

The sergeant, after Clark and Reynolds had calmed down, took matters in hand. He went to the track and came back with a small cinder. "Here," he said, handing it to Clark. "Put this in your right hand. Now, it's in your right hand. Right?"

Clark nodded.

"Say it. Go on. Say, 'It's in my right hand.'"

"It's in my right hand."

"Again. Say it over and over again."

"It's in my right hand. It's in my right hand. It's in my right hand."

"Good. That's enough. You can fall in. All right, Lieutenant, they're all yours."

Reynolds, red-faced and humiliated, marched us off. "Column right, march!" he shouted and Clark turned right. "Column left, march!" he shouted and Clark turned left. "Column right, march!" he shouted and Clark turned left.

"It's all right," said Sergeant Masters. "You have to be patient. Now Thornwell, which hand is the cinder in?"

He strained. His face turned red. His eyes were large blurs behind the thick glasses. "The right," he said.

"Good. Okay, try again."

And so it went, over and over again until Sergeant Masters, as Reynolds stood by with a smirk on his face, grabbed Clark by the shoulders and shook him. "What is it? What the hell is the matter?"

And Clark said, "I just can't remember which hand it's in."

Clark could remember other things: to get up in the morning, to eat breakfast. He could remember how to add and subtract and I even heard him recite a poem in class. He remembered the names of his classmates and teachers. And since like the rest of us he walked to school, he must have remembered which way to turn at various intersections. He wasn't the most brilliant student, but he wasn't the stupidest either; at least he seemed to pass all his courses. Today I suppose we would say he had a learning disability and forbid the military from discriminating against him for not being able to march. But the world wasn't so simple in the fifties; we hadn't learned to reduce our mysteries to pseudoscience.

Certainly we enjoyed watching him destroy Reynolds, and that he didn't seem to know what he was doing made the destruction even more enjoyable. But it also made Clark a simpleton. We laughed as hard at him as we laughed at Reynolds. But he never seemed to mind our laughter; he just went on staring wide-eyed through his thick glasses. Finally Clark was removed from the platoon and twice a week he went to Sergeant Masters's office and checked the attendance rolls, a job that took about ten minutes. The rest of the time he sat in the warm office, propped his feet up on the desk and watched us drill. Stupidity, we were forced to admit, has its rewards.

But we didn't want to be Clark. He might not have to march but he would also never have a girl, excel at a sport or have a decent job. Sometimes in the afternoon, when a group of us stood in the archway laughing and joking and shoving and shouting at the girls, I saw him walking away by himself and I felt sorry for him. I imagined his lonely afternoons and evenings, his great desire to be a part of the group. He wasn't a part of any group—not the athletes or the eggheads or even the photography club. And he certainly wasn't one of Miss Wagner's protégés. But there was nothing I could do; we had nothing in common.

Miss Wagner never apologized for her enigmatic explosion; she never even mentioned it. One day just before school let out for the Christmas holidays she asked me to remain after class. She stood in her favorite place, leaning on the window sill and staring out. "I want you to join the Latin Club and the Pen Pushers," she said. The Pen Pushers was a club for aspiring writers.

I suppose I looked down at the floor and said nothing.

"You don't want to join?"

"No. I don't. I mean, I like Latin. And I like to write but . . ."

"But you're afraid of what others will think of you if you join. Because of the kind of people who are in those clubs. Am I right?"

I didn't answer.

"All right. It's your decision."

"But I'll still be in your English class. And I'll go on with Latin."

She shook her head. "No, you can't be in my English class. I won't have you. You'll have to take Mrs. Hamilton

130

next year. And I'll recommend that you drop Latin because you're not advanced enough to continue."

"But you can't . . ."

"Oh, yes, I can." Her face wasn't red, no veins were bulging, her voice was calm. And yet I sensed a deep smoldering anger. Not disappointment. Anger.

"All right," I said and I turned away.

"You have to decide. You have to decide now. If not, you won't be anything. You'll just . . . drift. Until you drift into whatever the world wants you to be."

I came very close to accepting what she said, not because of what she taught or what I learned from her about books and writers but because of what *she* was, the way she moved, the way she waved her free hand about as she sat perched on the edge of her desk and read to us. *She* was like nothing at North Fulton High. To betray her was to betray a way of life.

And yet I sensed that she was reaching out to me because she needed something, because in some vital way she wasn't free, that she was trapped, too. Maybe not by a family of failures and eccentrics as I thought I was, but trapped by something. Whatever it was, it was intensified by the season. All around me were happy images of the most implausible faces gathered around huge food-filled tables and Christmas trees. The great windows in the department stores were filled with mechanical scenes: cobbler elves whose arms went up and down at the same time that the reindeer's heads bobbed down and up and Mrs. Santa's foot pressed and released the treadle on the sewing machine. A wonderful mechanized dance you saw by rubbing your breath off the cold glass. And the carols and hymns blared out of the old loudspeakers—scratchy and distorted—and the lights that illuminated the figures were bright and soft at the same time, the reds and blues and greens diffused by the frosty panes.

I marveled at the mysterious invention that had gone into the making of it all. Just as the distortion of the music and the erratic lighting were converted by my imagination into a reality as vivid as the steam radiators that hissed in my house or the icy bottles of milk I picked up from the front porch each morning. It was all a fantasy you could *understand* even as you believed it. The end of an age.

And my mother, too, was the end of an age, the last of her kind: a housewife who didn't know exactly what "being a housewife" meant beyond creating a world no less real than the worlds that went 'round and 'round and up and down in the store windows. Unlike Miss Wagner, she hardly seemed the person for creating worlds. And yet there was something similar about them. They were both thin and pale, with large dark eyes that somehow contradicted a small mouth. Of course, when I looked at her what I saw was a mother just as she was merely a daughter-in-law to my grandmother. And was she anything more than a wife to my father? Though he touched her, put his arm around her shoulders every now and then, patted her as she stood at the sink, he never seemed to . . . make contact with her. But sometimes when she paused and shut off the vacuum cleaner for a moment or when she stood at the sink and stared out the window, she seemed very like Miss Wagner, standing at the window and staring out at the schoolyard.

I suppose all the other houses in my neighborhood, as well as all the houses in all such neighborhoods — houses that had their own housewives and children and mothers-in-law and absentee fathers — were transformed by Christmas trees in the living room windows, trees illuminated by strings of large thick light bulbs and strings of popcorn and icicles and, here and there, actual little flickering candles. And electric candles in the windows and large wreaths on the doors. It was cumbersome, awkward. Like the mechanical scenes in the store windows. What mattered were the colors, the shapes. Even in the most fashionable neighborhoods in the city, people put huge Santa Claus sleigh scenes complete with reindeer on their roofs and strung oak and elm trees with lights. It was against that backdrop of gaudiness and vulgarity that I and my mother, last child and housewife of the Old Age, played out our little Christmas scene.

She stood by me, staring into the department store window at the little men and women and animals — chipmunks and rabbits and squirrels and deer — and a train, an old steam locomotive, weaving through it all. The clothes were Victorian — the thick, long full dresses on the women, the high hats and collars on the men. It was late afternoon, almost dark, and the rush hour crowds had gathered at the bus stops and the cars stood in long lines up and down the streets. It was less than a week until Christmas, until the actual day, the actual morning. My eyes moved from Santa and his elves, from Dickensian men bringing presents through swirling snow to Dickensian women — my eyes moved from that century to my own, to my mother in her hat with the fringe falling down over her forehead and the black coat with the fur collar and the skirt falling from beneath the coat halfway between her knees and ankles, halfway down to her black high-heel shoes. Behind her the dark gray cold Atlanta December seemed an extension of the display window.

"Come on," she said. "We have to get home."

Why? I wondered since my father wouldn't be home for hours. The house required no routine, especially now, when my sister and my brother and I weren't in school.

Yet the routine—the order my mother created—had to continue.

We turned and started down the sidewalk toward the bus stop. And then she saw him: a tall lanky man with a hat pushed back on his head, a cigarette hanging out of his mouth. He was dark, swarthy. Beside him on the sidewalk was a cart and on it were stacked several dozen little cardboard boxes. He was holding something in his hand, winding up whatever it was, and when we looked down at the pavement we saw what he was winding up: scurrying about, starting and stopping and rising up on their hind legs, were several little mechanical dogs. They were at once very lifelike and very mechanical and the combination made them very cute. But what really made them cute was their bark, a sharp, high-pitched "Yap! Yap!" that seemed to come first from one, then from another, according to no pattern or routine.

"Aren't they adorable?" my mother said. She stood and stared. "I've never seen anything like it. Listen to them bark."

"Why don't you buy one?"

She hesitated.

"How much are they?" I shouted to the man.

"Normally, a buck. To the lady, seventy-five cents."

"That's cheap," I said to my mother. "Go ahead."

"Seventy-five cents." She paused. "No. Let's go."

"But why not? You like them."

She put her head close to mine. "You never buy anything from a street vendor," she whispered. "They're mostly con men. They sell stolen goods."

"But how can he cheat you on these little dogs? And so what if he—"

"And if anything goes wrong, you can't return it. You'll never see him again."

"All right. So everything you say happens. What have you lost? Seventy-five cents."

But already she had me by the arm and was pulling me away.

"All right, fifty cents then," the man said and held out one of his boxes. And at his feet the little dogs whirled about, their "Yap! Yap!" splitting the air.

I couldn't read what was in my mother's eyes but it was something akin to panic. "No," she said. "Come on. We have to get away."

"Get away? Get away from what?"

"I mean, we have to get home." She paused. "Something will go wrong. I *know* it." She paused again. "Listen to that little bark. It's the cutest thing."

"Aw, come on. Buy one."

She took her little coin purse out of her handbag, opened it and stared into it for a moment. Then she took out two quarters. "There," she said. "I'll take one."

She practically snatched the box from him. "Come on, we'll be late." And at the bus stop she said, "I shouldn't have done it. I shouldn't have." For a moment I thought she would take it back, but then the bus swooped down and gathered us up.

My mother fidgeted through supper. She was nervous, giddy like a child. Why doesn't she just show them, I thought, but my father wasn't home yet and she had made me promise not to say anything. While we were eating dessert, he came in. He ate slowly.

"Hurry up," she said. "I have something to show you."

"What?"

"It's a surprise."

He grunted and went on eating slowly. My brother passed through the room, heading for the front door.

"Wait," she said. "Where are you going?"

"I have a date."

"Don't go yet. I have something to show you."

"But I'll be late."

"It won't take a minute. Hurry up, Calvin."

But my father didn't hurry up and my brother shifted from foot to foot and looked at his watch. And I thought, why is she making such a big thing of it?

Finally my father finished and she called us all into the living room. I sat with my sister on the sofa, my father sat in the old easy chair, my grandmother sat in the rocker and my brother stood by the door, ready to dart out. My mother stood in the middle of the room.

"Look," she said and she opened the box and held the dog over her head.

"It's a dog," my sister said.

"Isn't it cute?"

"Now watch." She wound the dog up and set it on the floor. It moved a few inches forward, whirled about, reared up, fell to its forepaws and started the cycle again. My mother and I looked at each other.

"It's real cute."

"How much did you pay for it?"

My mother stared at the dog, her face filled with confusion. "It's supposed to bark. When they were running around on the sidewalk, they were all barking."

"Sidewalk? You mean you bought it from somebody on the sidewalk?"

She picked up her dog and looked at it. She shook it and put it back on the floor. We all watched and waited but the only sound it made was a grinding noise.

"Well, I hope you didn't pay much for it?" my father said. "I thought you knew better than to buy from somebody on the street. I mean, I could understand if he bought it." He nodded toward me. "He's a kid. But you . . ."

My grandmother rose from her rocker. "The man was a ventriloquist. It's the oldest trick in the world."

"I have to go," my brother said and he darted out the door before anyone could stop him.

"But . . . he was smoking and they still barked."

"They can do it while they're eating and drinking. Any child knows that. I have to go do the dishes."

And then my sister said that she had "something to do" and went to her room. My father stood up, stretched. "Well, you can kiss that money goodbye. You'll never see that guy again."

"It only cost fifty cents," she said.

"Fifty cents is fifty cents."

And then there were only myself and my mother. She was still standing in the middle of the room; I was still sitting on the sofa. And between us the little dog ran and whirled and wheeled slower and slower. Finally the grinding noise died away and the dog stopped in midrear, his front paws in the air.

The lights from the Christmas tree illuminated her. She stood there, still as the tree itself, her white blouse the color of snow. She said, "They treat me like a child."

Words are solid, as solid as smells and sights. Nature may change from instant to instant so that no two days and no two Christmases are ever the same because no tree or flower or person remains the same from one instant to the next. But words are as lasting as Christmas lights and Victorian ladies and gentlemen and elves at cobblers' benches. And I need only hear those words of my mother— "They treat me like a child" —to see her exactly as she was then, trembling on the very edge of becoming what they treated her like. Her eyes grew moist. But then, miraculously . . .

"It was *your* fault."

"What?"

"Yes, it was you. You talked me into it."

I looked at her. She was smiling. No, it was more than that. Her eyes were sparkling. "You." She pointed at me.

"You didn't have to. You could have . . ."

"I'll never trust you again. Did you see the looks on their faces?" Now her voice *was* trembling, beginning to crack, but not with tears. "Did . . . you see them?" And then she was laughing. And I was laughing, too. "A . . . a ventriloquist . . . Yip! Yip! . . . Like . . . like this . . ."

She wound the dog up and as it scurried about she tried to keep her lips pressed together as she barked. And then I barked.

"Did you see your father? Did you?" She pulled herself up to full height, put a stern expression on her face and said, "'Fifty cents is fifty cents.' Now that's what I call *wisdom*." And she burst out laughing again.

At that moment I felt safe, secure. There was something about her laughter . . . the kind of laughter Minnie could never find, could only cackle in the smoke. The kind of laughter that eluded Luther, and, I was soon to discover, Allen as well. The kind of laughter that negates, for a moment at least, all the tyrannies of life. Only for a moment. But a moment is all we need. . .

Two days later we went to the drugstore in Buckhead and there in front of the Cokesbury Bookstore he stood, the little dogs barking at his feet.

"Look," I said, pointing at him. We were standing across the street. "There he is."

At first she was as surprised as I was. "My goodness. You're right." She chuckled. "Well, your father was wrong about that."

"I'll go home and get the dog, and we'll get our money back."

It would have been easy enough. We lived less than a mile away. But my mother, after staring at the man for a moment, shook her head. "No," she said. "Don't go to the trouble."

"But it's no trouble. I can be—"

"No," she said again and shook her head more insistently. "Leave him alone."

"Well, we ought to at least warn the others." A small crowd, mostly women, had gathered around him. "He'll cheat them like he cheated you."

Maybe she smiled. I don't know. I like to think she did, just before she said, "He didn't really cheat me."

-5-

Shortly after school began following the holidays a rumor began to circulate: Miss Wagner was going to marry Sergeant Masters. Like almost everyone else I didn't believe it at first; and even after it became more than a rumor, even after other teachers confirmed it, I still didn't believe it. But finally she confirmed it herself, told us in class that it was true. In typical fashion, she joked about it. "Yes, Mr. Masters has been mastered by my purity. I am his true Beatrice, destined to be his guide through the spheres."

And I thought, Sergeant Masters? Coach Murphy's punching bag.

As we were leaving the classroom, Marilyn muttered, "My purity . . ." and then her voice trailed off.

She was as irritating a presence as she had ever been and she spoke no more away from Vicki than she had spoken when she was with her. So I was surprised.

"What? What did you say?"

"I wasn't talking to you. I was talking to myself."

"But what did you say?"

Her voice rose. "I said, 'My purity, my ass.' There. You satisfied?"

Shocked as I was, I knew what she meant. I had thought of it when the rumor about the marriage first started to make the rounds. But I tried to bury it. Just as I tried to bury the truth about Vicki, that she wouldn't see me anymore, that she was actually going out on dates. Late into the night I tried not to imagine what she was doing on those dates. But the words of her friend, "My purity, my ass," kept running through my mind. What little I had, it seemed, was being taken away from me.

And then, one cold Sunday morning in February when I was delivering papers, I lost a little bit more.

I hated the route and was about to give it up under the pretense of needing more time for basketball. Sundays, however, weren't so bad; at least there was no danger that I would run into any of my friends at six o'clock in the morning. But one morning I did run into Clark.

I was at the end of my route. My hands were stiff and red beneath the black newsprint; my face and feet were aching and my breath poured out of my mouth in a great cloud of mist. And then, as I turned a corner, I saw someone crawling out the ground floor back window of a house. A burglar, I thought and was wondering what I should do when I realized that the person was Clark Thornwell. Clark a burglar? I couldn't believe it. Who lived in the house? Of course. Marilyn's family. And sure enough, when Clark was safely on the ground, mousy little Marilyn herself leaned out the window and kissed him. At first I couldn't take it all in; I had kissed Vicki, I had even groped about a bit in dark rooms. But Clark was coming out of a bedroom window at sunrise. And just about the time I figured out what that meant, he turned and saw me standing there, staring at him. It was an awkward moment and all he could do was come to me and all I could do was wait for him. He was smiling. "Hi," he said.

"Hi."

"You won't tell anybody, will you?"

"No. No, I won't tell." And indeed I wouldn't, though if it had been myself coming out that window, I think I would have told the world. But never would I humiliate myself enough to reveal what was simply impossible about Clark's life. Why in the world didn't he want anybody to know? Why didn't he tell everybody?

"You must be about through. When you finish up we'll go for a ride."

"A ride? What do you mean?"

"Oh, I've got a car. I always use a car on Sundays when there's no traffic."

Use a car? We were only fourteen.

And the car turned out to be a T-Model Ford.

"It's Dad's. He runs a repair place. He's a mechanic. He keeps this one running and lets me drive it sometimes. It's not like modern cars. You have to spark it and other things. It's a lot of fun."

The car coughed and spit and sputtered and then rattled along the silent streets. At first I was afraid, but once it became obvious that Clark knew what he was doing—he seemed to have been driving for years—I relaxed and enjoyed myself.

We moved through a still and empty Buckhead and out West Paces Ferry past the mansions set back on their wooded estates. I looked at Clark. As he drove, the expression on his face didn't change—it was the same expression that he wore when he marched, when he sat in Sergeant Masters's office with his feet propped up on the desk, when he walked away from the school grounds alone, when he came out of Marilyn's window. The eyes wide and blurred by the thick lenses of his glasses. The expression of the bookworm, the egghead, riding above the short stocky body of the redneck, the clod.

"Let's go to the river!" I shouted.

"Okay! Which way?"

"Just go on across 41. I'll know the way when I get there."

Once we crossed the Marietta highway the land became almost rural; only an occasional house emerged from among the trees. It was light now, the first light of a clear February day, and the horizon was streaked with orange, a cold desolate but magnificent color rising out of the darkness. Probably I remember the morning and the weather so precisely because it was the first time I had been out in a car not driven by an adult. I felt free and the morning seemed a part of that freedom. So lost was I in my fantasy that the fork in the road was on me before I saw it.

"Which way?" Clark yelled.

"Left!"

He jerked the car in that direction, flinging me against the door.

"No!" I shouted. "I mean right! Right!"

And he jerked the car in that direction, flinging me against him. The car jumped the curb, ran for a moment along the shoulder, then dropped back onto the road. And we were heading for the Chattahoochee River.

"Sorry," I said. "I wasn't watching."

"That's all right. We made it."

Indeed we did. And it wasn't until we got to the river and pulled to a stop on a steep hill that fell into the water where the morning sunlight danced on the ripples and he had shut the engine off that it occurred to me exactly *how* we had made it. I looked at Clark and he seemed to know what I was thinking.

"Luck," he mumbled. "It was just luck."

I shook my head. In the great scheme of the universe luck was possible, but between us we knew that in this particular instance it was impossible. After the noise of the engine the silence was immense. We could hear the water far below as it broke over rocks and around fallen limbs of trees.

"You won't tell anybody, will you?"

It was the second time he had asked that question and for the second time I said, "No, I won't tell," even though I knew it would be much more difficult to keep this secret.

"Why?" I asked. "Why go to all the trouble?"

He shrugged.

"I mean, it would be a lot easier just to march. It's only a couple of hours a week."

"I don't mind marching."

"Then . . ." I stopped. Suddenly it dawned on me. "Christ," I muttered.

He looked at me and smiled. I could see the smile on his lips, on his cheeks. But his eyes remained the same: enormous blurs behind his glasses. It was the most chilling smile I had ever seen.

But the smile was no more chilling than the words of Miss Wagner the next afternoon. She stood by the window, the one hand resting beneath her breasts, the other fiddling with the venetian blind cord. She wasn't looking at me; she was staring out the window. "So you made your decision," she said.

I nodded.

"No Pen Pushers, no Latin Club."

I nodded again.

"That means no more Latin, no more English in my class."

"I know."

"All right. Have it your own way. You'll make good grades and you'll play football and you'll go off to college."

"What's wrong with that?"

"Nothing's *wrong* with it. Nothing's *right* with it either. I must say, I expected better of you. I thought you were a poet."

"You said my poem was insincere. You said *I* was insincere."

"It was and you are."

And before I knew it, I said — hissed, "And what about you?"

She turned and looked at me. "So there we have it. It's *my* fault. You just won't take responsibility for anything, will you?"

A long silence followed and I suspect she was just about to tell me to leave and probably I sensed as much and managed to squeeze out one word: "Why?"

Her eyes searched mine for a moment and then shifted back to the window. "What else is there for me?" she asked, but it wasn't really a question. "A home. Children. That's the way . . . You know what I mean."

But I didn't. Or rather, we weren't talking about the same thing and it was impossible for me to get out of myself, to listen to her. She twirled the cord with her fingers and stared out through the bars the wood around the panes formed. "Henry is sweet. I know he . . . he doesn't seem . . ." Suddenly she stopped. "My goodness, what am I talking to you this way for? You have betrayed me. Betrayed and abandoned me. What do you care what I do? What do I care what you think? Go on. Get out of here. Never darken my door again."

"It's not him," I said. "Not Sergeant Masters."

"Then what is it?"

I tried to speak, tried to say it. But I didn't know how. She was right. I had no business talking to her about it. But I could see Clark crawling out of that bedroom, could see Vicki standing in the window that hot afteroon. And I squeezed out the name: "Coach Murphy."

"Oh, my God," she whispered.

And just as I couldn't ask the question, she couldn't answer it. The image of Vicki disappeared to be replaced by that of my mother, standing in the living room, staring down at the little mechanical dog. It was unbearable but before I could break she said, "Someday you'll understand."

With those words she became for me just another teacher, just another adult. Yet even at the time I sensed that that was what she intended and in a way that was her real lesson, the most important thing she taught: that "style" is what we develop in order to keep from inflicting our own suffering upon others. Because she said something as trite, as condescending as "Someday you'll understand," I could say, "Yeah, sure, that's what my mother always says," and walk out of the room and out of her life.

Not long after that day Clark's family moved. Clark didn't tell anyone. At least I don't guess he did; I had become no friendlier with him than I had been before that Sunday morning. One day someone noticed that he wasn't around anymore; maybe that was the day he left, maybe he'd been gone for days or weeks. Of course, Marilyn was still around. Occasionally I passed her in the hall and each time I wondered whether or not she had seen me that morning. She seemed far less mousy than she had been before I saw her leaning out the window and, youth being what it is, I finally made a move and asked her if she'd like to "go out" sometime. Her eyes, unlike Clark's, were clear, direct and unobscured by glasses and her stare went right through me as she said, "I wouldn't go out with you if you were the last bastard on earth." So I figured that maybe she had seen me that morning. And I also figured that she didn't much care whether or not I told anyone about it. Of course, I didn't. Just as I didn't

147

tell anyone about Clark's marching. At the time I may have convinced myself otherwise, but now I know that I wasn't protecting anyone's reputation or shielding anyone from reprisal. No, I simply couldn't bear to admit to anyone the reality of what I had discovered about Clark, about Marilyn and — most of all — about myself.

Clark was gone, Vicki was gone, Miss Wagner was gone. Everybody, it seemed, could get away but me. And then I discovered that Allen was gone.

"He hasn't been here?" asked Uncle Thad. His large stomach spilled over his belt; his huge red face was heavily lined, the eyes, green and set deep beneath the brows, were blank. He was tall but not nearly as tall as his son. By his side stood his wife, Aunt Molly, her eyes moist, her pale cheeks streaked with tears.

"Not for days," said my mother. "Maybe he's staying with friends."

"Friends!" Uncle Thad snorted. "He doesn't have any friends. Or if he has made any, I sure as hell hope he's not with 'em."

"Oh, Margaret, you don't suppose he's hurt, do you?" wailed Aunt Molly.

My mother put her arm around her. Uncle Thad shrugged and said, "Maybe he's just taken off again."

No, I thought. He wouldn't have. And I blurted out, "Not without telling me. He wouldn't have left without telling me."

My mother, alarmed, looked at me but said nothing.

Later that night my father did. He called Allen shiftless, lazy, good-for-nothing, a loafer, a misery to his parents. My mother tried to soften the tirade with words about being poor, personal difficulties, the inevitability of certain things — an attempt at moral balancing that my father would have none of. "I told you that we shouldn't have let him come around so much," he said. "Damn it, I told you."

"But he didn't have anywhere else to go. And besides, our boy's not like him. Just because he likes him doesn't mean . . ."

"I don't want you seeing him anymore," he said to me.

"Why shouldn't I see him? What's wrong with him?"

My father didn't answer but our eyes locked and I knew that my parents knew something that they couldn't, or wouldn't, tell me. Not now, at any rate. But I felt that my father was biding his time.

The wind roared through the trees. ("No wonder he's gone," I told my mother that morning. "Look at Uncle Thad." And my mother—first surprised, then amused—said, "Uncle Thad wouldn't hurt a fly.") The sky was a deep blue, a winter sky filled with a sun that was bright but not hot. ("He was wearing a gun . . . and just look at him." "He has to wear a gun, he's a security guard, but that doesn't mean anything. Lord, the things I've seen him do for that boy. They've tried everything.") The dead leaves, crumbling, swirled around me. The wind stung my face. ("I'd leave too if he was my father." And she said, "I know that he looks mean, but he's not. Things aren't always what they look like. He's just a tired old man." And I thought: *A fat tired old man with a gun*.)

Dark clouds were gathering in the western sky as I passed in front of Sam's Bar. The odor of beer and greasy food wafted onto the street. I gazed into the semi-darkness at the men propped against the bar, hoping to make out the shape of Allen, but he wasn't there. What do they do when they leave? I wondered. Do they ever leave?

Had I ever seen the same face twice? Had I ever seen any but these faces?

I moved along the busy street, then down the hill along by the stream and finally I came to the bank overlooking the basketball court. A group of boys saw me and motioned to me to come down and join in their game. I stood and stared at them, feeling the wind grow stronger on the back of my neck. I looked up. The clouds on the horizon had expanded and almost half the sky had grown dark.

That night the rain came down in torrents and the wind whipped the great oaks about like bamboo shoots. I lay in bed and stared at the ceiling and wondered if I could leave unless I went with Allen. Not physically, but . . . how? What did it matter if he had already left? Allen was a phantom in the rainstorm, one of the faces at the bar where the men sat even as the storm raged outside.

All the next day the rain fell out of the dark sky, driven about by strong shifting winds. It pounded against the window as I ate breakfast, it slanted down by the classroom windows, beat against the metal roof of the gym as I practiced with the rest of the team, streaked the dining room windows as I ate supper with my father, who cursed what it was doing to the houses he was trying to build while my mother murmured that "the farmers need it," causing my grandmother to reminisce about her days growing up on the farm. My brother gulped great quantities of milk and said nothing. My sister, pale and ill, picked at her food. Our faces ringed the table and for a moment I felt that I was outside the circle, their words didn't seem to reach, to touch me; but when I looked out the rain-streaked window at the wall of darkness, I felt the circle close tight around me and I was glad after dinner to climb the stairs early and lie alone in the bed. Alone with

Allen, the two of us drifting through strange towns and great stretches of farm land and mountains as I drifted off into sleep.

Somewhere far away the telephone was ringing. The rain ticked against the windowpanes. The room was dark. The telephone rang and rang. Grandmother wouldn't answer it, my sister would be afraid, my father slept like a dead man and my mother was probably lying on her good ear. I made my way down the stairs, through the dining room and got to the hall just as my father picked up the receiver.

"All right, Molly, calm down. What is it?"

Silence.

"Well, call the police."

Then the wails of Molly echoed down the hall. My father had to remove the receiver from his ear.

"Molly, it'll take me forever to get there. Call the police."

The wails again and the recurring phrases, ". . . only you! . . . please come! . . . you! . . ."

"All right, all right. But please . . . All right, I'm coming!"

He hung up and then noticed that I was there, standing in my underwear in the hall. He stared at me for a moment. "Damn it, get dressed. You're coming with me. It'll do you good."

"What is it?" my mother called from the bedroom.

"Allen. He's at it again."

"Oh, my God . . ."

I scrambled up to my room, my heart pounding with fear and excitement. As I dressed I could hear my parents arguing below, their words rising through the silent house.

"He's too young. He shouldn't go."

151

"Oh, hell, to you he'll always be too young."

"Please, Calvin."

"No. You know the way he is. We've got to snap him out of it."

"But no . . ."

The bedroom door slammed and I was dressed and standing at the foot of the stairs and my father passed by me and said, "Come on."

The streets, wet and glistening beneath the streetlights, were deserted. The windshield wiper moved back and forth, knocking the rain away, and from time to time the car was rocked by pools of water. In the business district the tops of the buildings vanished in the darkness above the streetlights. Five Points, the heart of the city and the outer limit of my own roaming, was deserted (except for the statue of Henry Grady, his chest thrown out against the weather). Then we moved into sections I knew nothing about, the old fashionable residential areas, once considered elegant because of their gables and scrolls and turrets, now slum dwellings for black families. My father talked almost constantly, half to himself, half to me, trying to point out "the lesson" in what was happening.

"Allen gets drunk, goes on benders. He tries to beat up his father. Sometimes his mother . . . Happens time and again . . . Best thing ever happened, his going away . . . Don't know why he came back . . . Oh, he's got his reasons. I don't suppose he can help the way he is."

"You mean his drinking? Does he drink too much?"

"Yes. No. I mean he does but that isn't what . . . Never mind. Anyway, what I'm saying is, this isn't the first time I've had to go . . . God almighty, I don't know why they don't just toss him out and be done with it. I know he can't help . . ."

The dark houses, the wet glistening empty streets, the pools of water, the windshield wipers going back and forth, back and forth. Almost the same route I took with my mother when we went to see Minnie only now I couldn't see the barren blackberry thickets, the rusting hulks of cars, the scrawny dogs. And then the factory came into view, enormous, sprawling over several acres, lights here and there flashing in the darkness, a trail of smoke curling up against the dark sky. Row after row of small dingy white wood houses, workers' houses. My father stopped the car in front of one of them, the only one on the block that was lighted. Molly's wailing filled the air and I wondered, Where are the neighbors? I followed my father up the muddy path to the door. He didn't knock. He pushed the door open and light broke over us. We entered the room.

Molly was on her knees beside Allen. He lay on his side by a pool of blood that was still oozing from his body. One arm was beneath him, the other was thrown over his head. His legs were a grotesque tangle. Across the room, by the small mantle, stood Uncle Thad, a shotgun in his hands. Molly turned slightly when the door opened. "He's dead!" she screamed. "He's dead!"

"What happened?" asked my father.

Uncle Thad's eyes were blank and his lips seemed to move independent of his jaws, his face, his mind. "He came in drunk, he took the gun off the wall, I tried to get it away from him and it went off."

"He's dead!"

"He took the gun off the wall, I tried to get it away from him and it went off," Uncle Thad said again, his eyes now fixed on the gun.

"He killed him!" Molly screamed. "O Lord! He killed my baby!"

I forced myself to look at the body again, the long body that stretched almost from wall to wall in that tiny room. And my mind echoed Aunt Molly's words. He killed him, I thought, again and again. The fat son-of-a-bitch killed him. And strange to say, as the words hammered against my brain I felt a sense of ecstasy, of release such as I had felt for an instant as I sat at the dinner table, the rain pecking against the window. Then hands were on my shoulder, shaking me, and my father's face was directly in front of mine, only inches away. "Snap out of it!"

"What?"

"The police. Call the police."

As I looked around the room, trying to find the telephone, I saw Uncle Thad. He was still standing by the mantle, his eyes filled with tears, tears that streamed down his cheeks, over his jaws. He turned his eyes to the ceiling. "God! God!" he cried and in an instant he twisted the shotgun in his hands, held the trigger and butt away from him, and jammed the barrel against his temple.

"No!" Molly screamed, the word almost lost in the wildness of her voice. "No!"

Sweat poured from his hair over his face and he held the barrel against his head with trembling hands.

"For God's sake, Thad," said my father in a low voice. He was frozen, as I was frozen, afraid even the slightest movement would tighten the finger on the trigger.

"I'm sorry," Molly pleaded. "I didn't mean it. He was my baby, but it wasn't your fault. You couldn't . . ."

But her words couldn't stop the finger as it drew the trigger back.

Afterwards I would believe that I heard the rain falling outside, that image after image — the bar, the dinner table, the afternoons by the stream, basketball games—flashed through my brain, that I heard the explosion, saw the side of Uncle Thad's head blown off—all in an instant. Even now, as I write, I still believe I saw all that though I know that what I actually heard was a click, a click that echoed through the small room more loudly than any blast could have.

Uncle Thad, his eyes still squeezed shut, held the gun against his head for several moments before he realized what had happened. When he opened them, they blazed with a mixture of bewilderment and rage. "It's empty," he said as he lowered it from his head. "Empty," he repeated as though he was stating a profound impossibility.

I stood between the body on the floor and the one by the mantle and felt the circle of utter silence draw me in, a silence stretching out into the dark rain, forward into the farthest reaches of my life, a silence not broken by the sobs of my uncle as he fell to his knees, not broken by my father's whisper, "Call the police, Son," not broken, either circle or silence, by my movement toward the telephone, which I knew was the "lesson"—that this movement like all others was made in silence, in the ring of blank faces which included not only myself and Molly and Uncle Thad and my father but also the long, dead body of Allen.

As I walked to school the day after we buried Allen in the longest coffin I've ever seen, I passed an old fading poster that was stapled to a telephone pole and stopped and stared at it. The fatherly face dissolved into Clark's smile, a smile that would come back to me again and again, especially when I encountered—first in one country, then in another—the grand rhetoric of history and philosophy, the idolization of men and events. I would see that face when, alone in my room, I read books that pulled the crooked terrain of the past into a straight line; when, jostled by crowds, I watched the flailing arms and pointing fingers of politicians. But it was Allen's voice I heard when I read aloud the slogan, "I Like Ike."

PART
3
1955-56

For then we played for victory
And not to make each other glad.
A darkness covered every head,
Frowns twisted the original face
And through that mask we could not see
The beauty and the buried grace.

—Edwin Muir

Uncle Luther and my mother and father and grand-mother and Uncle Walter are in the living room. I'm not supposed to hear them; I'm supposed to be studying in the dining room but I can see into the living room. I'm not supposed to know about Luther either, that he got thrown into jail for trying to rob a liquor store, that at the trial the judge suspended his sentence because of his war record but insisted that he go into a V.A. hospital for "treatment." It is a hot steamy summer night and the windows are open and my parents probably think I can't hear what's being said over the hum of the attic fan.

"It's best, Luther."

"They know how to treat cases like yours. You can't go on like this."

"I don't want to go back. I've been in the hospital. It don't do no good."

"It's that or jail." Then Uncle Walter realizes he's broken the tone of the conversation and goes quickly on. "And when you come out, I'll have a job waiting for you."

"I don't know nothing but plastering and painting."

"It's never too late to learn. That's one thing I know. You have to experiment, change, make the best of things. That's been the key to my career. Look at Calvin here. He was a house painter and now he's a builder."

"I'm too old."

"You're never too old to change."

"It's not your fault," my mother says. "You've got to realize that. Let them help you."

"It's not charity," my father says. "You gave every-thing for your country. Now they owe you something. We all do."

Luther slumps back on the sofa. His eyes fill with tears. "All right. All right, I'll do it."

My mother puts her arms around him and holds him. "You'll never regret it."

"No sirree."

And then my grandmother's voice booms through the room. "It's your own fault!"

The room grows so silent the crickets outside become a screaming chorus.

"Ill." My grandmother's voice is filled with sarcasm. "You just don't have any willpower, that's all. When you want to stop being a drunkard, you will."

"Kate!"

"Oh, it's none of my business, I know. It's not my family, it's yours." She is staring at my mother. "But I've lived all my life with people who drink too much." Her gaze shifts to my father, then Luther. "Self-pity, that's all. And worrying your family to death."

"Kate! Be quiet!"

She stands up. "Well, I've had my say."

-1-

On afternoons in early August we went to the vast vacant lot at the corner of Lenox and Peachtree because we knew that somehow the blacks would know we were there. And they always showed up, emerging from Johnsontown, a mysterious enclave on the other side of Lenox that probably developed as a place for the servants who worked in the mansions along West Paces Ferry and Habersham. Dressed in garish old T-shirts and baggy pleated shorts and ragged tennis shoes, they spoke a language we mimicked but could barely understand.

The one thing we all understood was football. The games began civilly, each side recognizing the fact that we were playing *touch* football without pads or helmets. But gradually, as our feet smashed the few scraggly weeds and kicked up dust from the rock hard red clay—dust that hung suspended in humid air and clogged our lungs and turned our sweat gritty—gradually touch became push and push became slap and hand became forearm. And before we knew it, we were playing tackle, were crashing against each other's bodies. It was much rougher than anything we would experience when we started playing real games in the fall. And strange to say, we threw ourselves into these games. There were no cheering crowds, no parents to impress, no cheerleaders or girlfriends, no college scouts—nothing beyond the game itself. It mattered to no one but the players who won or lost, and finally it didn't even matter to the players. We cared about nothing but the next run, the next pass, the next tackle.

I can't say that our two worlds—the black world and the white world—came together, merged in that vacant lot. For an hour or two we moved outside both worlds, but when it was over—when somebody said, "Damn, it's six o'clock" or we heard a woman's voice from across the road calling an unfamiliar name, and we stood, sweaty and grimy and scratched and bruised, and faced each other for a moment and maybe even shook hands before we began to trickle away—nothing had changed. They fell into a group, crossed Lenox Road and disappeared into Johnsontown.

And waiting for us, leaning against one of his old cars, was Cal. Overweight, dumpy, with sagging shoulders and chest and stomach and short legs. When he moved, he shuffled in a duck-footed walk as though he were trying to make the earth and not his feet absorb his weight.

At least, that's how I remembered him when, thirty years later, sitting in an expensive Atlanta restaurant at two in the morning, I heard someone say, "They found him in a motel in some little town in Alabama. Found him on the bathroom floor."

"Who? Who're you talking about?"

"Cal."

"No. What was it?"

"Drugs, they say. An overdose. That's what I heard."

"When?"

"Oh, God, that was, let's see, ten, fifteen years ago."

I wondered why I hadn't noticed that Cal wasn't at the class reunion we had just come from but when the image of Cal standing next to the car drifted through my mind, I knew the answer: we never noticed when Cal wasn't there because we always knew where he was. And then I wondered why I remembered what he was like on that particular afternoon, why I remembered as well—and as vividly—that football game and the blacks. Cal never played football just as he never listened to rock-and-roll music but stuck to the "big bands." He always remained detached, somehow alien. This was partly because he was a Yankee. (Actually he was a midwesterner, from Illinois, but in Buckhead anyone from outside the South was a "Yankee.") He never lost his clipped nasal accent or cut his hair short. And he always drank beer. I think the first time I ever saw him, when he was fifteen years old and his family had just moved to Atlanta, he was standing in the high school parking lot with a bottle of beer in his hand. A strange sight since only the overalled farm boys from Sandy Springs had the courage — or the indifference — to drink beer on school property.

But paradoxically, because he didn't "fit in," he almost immediately did fit in and become a part of the group. I think we sensed from the first that Cal was genuine. He didn't seem to need the group. He was capable of disappearing for days — even weeks — at a time. Of course, we all knew where he disappeared to — to his backyard and his cars.

"He had a son," someone at the table said, bringing me back to the restaurant. "Got killed in Vietnam."

"He shouldn't have let him go," Billy said. Billy was another surprise — actually a shock. He had become a surgeon at one of the most famous medical centers on the West Coast.

"Wasn't much he could do. His wife raised him. Cal hardly ever saw him."

"Which wife? The first or second one?"

"Well, *somebody* should have kept him from going," Billy insisted, his expression reflecting his old inability to concentrate on more than one thing at once.

"Why? Why shouldn't he have gone?" An irritated voice. I felt the old battle being revived. I dreaded it.

Billy said, "I've been to countries in Asia and Africa and I didn't see anything there that would be worth my son's life."

What shocked me was not what Billy said but the way he said it. He spoke as he ate, and his tone of voice was a mixture of disgust and the matter-of-fact, as though whole races of people were worth no more than the bacon he was chewing. "If there was another war in any of those places or in Central or South America, I'd get him to Canada. I wouldn't let him go."

"How old is he?" I asked.

"He's twenty."

"Then how would you stop him if he wanted to go?"

"Wanted to go? He's twenty. Boys that age don't think with their heads, they think with their penis. I'd just tell him, 'Hell, no.' He'd get over it."

I thought of my own son, only twelve, not old enough to go off to war. But then I remembered myself when I was his age, how I feared the Korean War, and I thought, maybe he's afraid of things I don't even know about.

Billy wasn't there on those August afternoons. In fact, although I played on the high school basketball team with Billy and must have been with him every winter afternoon for years, not to mention all the games at night, I retain only one clear image of him. I mean, those flashes that come and go involuntarily, snapshots of childhood friends *in action*, doing something. If what we do is what we are, he exists in my past only in one basketball game.

And in August there was no basketball. Long ago I'd given up my make-believe games, so there was only the heat and the tail end of summer jobs and the brutal football games against the blacks. Cal, like Billy, never took part in those games, but he came and stood in the heat and watched and afterwards several of us piled into his car to be driven back to our homes and I watched those blacks trudging across Lenox Road to theirs. I had never seen their homes, the "place" they used, as we used ours,

to hold the outside world at bay for a few years. Sometimes I wanted to follow them across the road and down
into Johnsontown, but I felt that that would be a violation
of something.

Cal didn't always get us all the way home. Sometimes
we wound up walking partway because, though Cal was
obsessed with cars, with what they looked like and how
they ran, the ones he drove were notoriously unreliable.
Of course, car freaks were common in the fifties but once
again, Cal was different. In the South they tended to be
tobacco-chewing illiterates who managed to keep old
clunkers running for brief periods, who followed the
Flock brothers on the stockcar circuit and who went every
Friday night to the races at the Peach Bowl where good
old boys dodged the potholes and—sometimes—each
other as they went 'round and 'round the small oval. No,
for Cal the internal combustion engine was part of the
greater mystery of mass and movement. One of Newton's
last apostles, he was always searching for another ratio
that would give him even greater power over gravity and
friction and inertia. His cars ran perfectly or they ran not
at all. Consequently, they almost never ran. But that didn't
matter because they were always on the verge of
running—splendidly, magnificently.

"What do you want to do?" one of us would ask as we
drove around, bored.

"I don't know. Let's go see Cal."

When we pulled up in his yard, he was a pair of feet
sticking out from underneath the car or a pair of buttocks
protruding from a front fender, his upper body and head
lost beneath the raised hood. And always nearby, on a tool
box or tree stump or old tire, was an open, half-drunk
bottle of beer. He acknowledged our presence with

grunts and snatches of conversation but he never took his eyes or his mind off the engine he was tinkering with.

Often he cut school to work on it—or so he said. The truth was, he hated his studies about as much as he loved cars. He performed abysmally in English and history and foreign languages, none of which he ever studied. And he didn't study math or physics either, but in them he was absolutely perfect. He was, in fact, the only student in the history of North Fulton High who had ever been known to defeat Miss Lee.

At least, that was the legend. None of us could know about all Miss Lee's classes stretching back to 1930 when, tradition had it, builders found her sitting in the woods in the northern part of Fulton County and built the school around her. A stern and ominous woman, probably not nearly as old as we thought she was, she taught trig-onometry and college algebra and her obsession was form, technique. "Mathematics, like life itself, is ritual," she insisted. "The correct answer is not nearly as impor-tant as the method you use to achieve it." And there was only one method—hers. Gradually, over the course of a year, we learned never to take a shortcut, never to skip a step, never to get our columns of figures out of line. She was right, of course. Most of us were incapable of grasp-ing the abstract concepts of mathematics but we could, through careful attention to method, glimpse them from time to time and be assured that behind the pages of numbers we assembled there existed an order as firm and definite as Miss Lee herself.

Cal, however, would have none of it. He turned in papers (I saw several of them) that were simply chaotic: indecipherable columns of figures interspersed with lines and arrows; margins filled with numbers and equations written sideways; clumps of computation that seemed to have nothing to do with whatever the main train of calculation was — all smudged by his oily, greasy hands. And somewhere on the page, written large and contained within a heavily drawn circle, was the answer — invariably the correct answer.

What developed was a battle of wills. Miss Lee began by failing his papers over and over again. She kept him after school, wrote letters to his parents, even, in a fit of temper, sent him to the principal, who must have wondered how he was supposed to punish a student for getting the right answer in the wrong way.

"What did he say to you?" I asked Cal.

"He asked me if I couldn't do it my way, get the right answer and then use Miss Lee's method."

Sending him to the principal was an act of despair, the signal that Miss Lee was losing. Just before Christmas holidays she gave up. Probably she assumed he was a genius and would come to no good end. His papers began to come back devoid of any marks save a small A written in the upper left-hand corner. He made an A in trigonometry. After Christmas, when we turned to college algebra, she made one more futile attempt, gave him a couple of F's, and gave up once again.

But that was later. Now, in the fall of the year, I was engaged in rituals of my own, rituals that involved battles with other schools, battles over girls and, in an oblique way, battles with rats.

"They're in the kitchen now," my grandmother said.

She meant that the rats, that for some mysterious reason had appeared in the basement, had now moved up into the house. And my father, after insisting that she was wrong, found unmistakable signs that she was right. But then, he had begun by insisting that there were no rats at all. He never heard them and neither did my mother and they slept downstairs. How could my grandmother, who slept upstairs, possibly hear them? Maybe she intuited them. Or maybe she heard them on her night rambles when she couldn't sleep and came down to the living room to make sure that the clock was right. "It didn't chime three," she said, "so I knew something was wrong." Did she lie awake all night, waiting for the clock to chime the hour? The half hour?

Where did the rats come from? My father blamed them on the cheap apartments that had been crammed on the lot next door in such a way that the garbage cans were only a few feet from the side of our house. But we had had rats from time to time before the apartments were built. My mother blamed them on the damp basement with its dirt bank only partially sealed off by concrete blocks, another example of the shoddy work that my father, a builder, did on his own house. But during all those afternoons and evenings that I spent in my basement room I never saw a rat, and though other houses in the neighborhood had dirt basements, none of the neighbors seemed to have trouble with rats. My grandmother, of course, had her own ideas.

"Death," she said. "Death or disaster. That's what rats mean."

"Well, it can't be disaster," said my mother. "That's already happened."

She was referring to the fact that my father had finally overextended himself, gotten caught in the recession and been foreclosed on by the bank. That was why he was at home. That was why he could deal with the rats. "After all," he said, "I've been fighting rats for years." By which he meant the bankers. We could only hope that he would be more successful with the actual creatures.

For a while he wasn't. He descended into the basement and put traps everywhere. All through the night we
were awakened by traps snapping shut, but in the morning we found no rats in them. Sometimes I went into the
basement with him and then I remembered my old room.
It was gone now. All that remained were the bookcase
with its mildewed books and a single moth-eaten blanket
hanging from a nail in a rafter. For some reason no one
had ever bothered to pull it down: the ruins of my previous solitude given over to the crafty devious rats.

Above the basement, in the sunlight, Miranda rolled
and swayed like summer. Her round breasts and buttocks
bounced when she walked and I, who had worked in a
grocery store, knew that they would give slightly under
my fingers like fruit. Her skin, well into the fall, was a
deep rich even brown and her hair was silk, long and
thick and almost black. It caught the glare of the sun like
a smooth dark pond. But her lips were taut, seemed
always poised and powerful, between her plump cheeks.

Where she came from no one seemed to know. Some
said from Florida, others said from the mountains. She
simply appeared on the first day of class, an awesome
presence in the classroom, nymph amid the desks and
books and chalk dust. A prize. Something to be won or
lost. Even duck-footed Cal's head rose from his mysterious calculations to watch her walk into the room. And
Billy, who could ill afford any distraction in the classroom,
had an especially hard time. His face — the uncomprehending eyes, the nose and chin that seemed to come
together above his mouth, the constantly furrowed
forehead — suggested either intense concentration or stupidity. Or both, a kind of desperate effort to understand
the world around him. He was slow-witted, never volunteered any answers and when called upon invariably gave

the wrong answer. It wasn't that he didn't study. That, I think, was the reason that we didn't see much of him outside of school and sports—because, unlike the rest of us, he was studying. But he didn't have the resources to support two pursuits, academic and athletic. In fact, he didn't have the resources to support more than one sport, basketball. The last thing he needed before the season was Miranda.

And the last thing Billy could have was Miranda, because it was fall, football season, and as Miranda once confided in me, she liked "men of action." By that she meant football players. Our fullback Nick Cromsky seemed to think that she meant him. He often spoke of her in a vulgar way. But he was tall, thick and dark. His arms and legs were powerful beyond his years (although it was rumored that he was actually too old to be in high school, that he had lied about his age). There was a hard coldness about him that chilled everyone who knew him. And so we let him say what he pleased.

And always Billy hovered in the background, like a vulture, waiting. And even Cal, in his own way, tried. For maybe his yearlong battle against Billy Ray had something to do with Miranda. Which is another way of saying that his obsession with time, space and movement was in some way or another human.

We didn't know Billy Ray's last name or even where he came from. But we knew what he was—a redneck. He chewed tobacco, wore grimy uncuffed blue jeans and a soiled and torn T-shirt with the shirt sleeves rolled up over the shoulders. He had long greasy black hair, a cigarette stuck behind one ear, and bad teeth. We saw him only when we ventured out of the friendly environs of Buckhead to the Fairburn dragstrip. There once a month for almost a year Cal raced his car against Billy Ray's in a classification so esoteric only Billy Ray and Cal competed in it.

It was a classic confrontation between the two extremes of the machine age: the grubby illiterate descendent of dirt farmers who over generations had learned nothing about engines except what works versus the midwesterner who knew, without ever having learned it, why an engine works, and sought to develop it according to the equations in his brain. How could he know that Newton's universe favored the ignorant believer who accepted without question the limits of metal and fire? That Euclid, only one of an infinite number of possibilities, had been pushed to his limits, that already another model was challenging the reality of speed itself. All he knew was that month after month he lost, month after month Billy Ray grasped the small trophy in his hands and grinned, exposing his rotten teeth.

But Cal seemed unflappable. He took each defeat as well as our ribbing in stride.

"Getting ready for old Billy Ray?" we'd ask him when we found him leaning into his engine. Or, in the halls of the school, we'd sneak up behind him, go, "Vrooom, vrooom!" and say, "It's Billy Ray closing in on you" or "There goes Billy Ray." He didn't seem to mind.

We thought, considering that Cal was a genius, that maybe his driving was at fault. Certainly when he took us on wild rides (always in his father's car) through the winding downhill stretch of Peachtree-Dunwoody Road, he didn't always seem to have control of the car; sometimes in breathtaking moments the car seemed to spin him through the curves rather than the other way around. But when he hit the long straight stretch that cut through what was still a horse farm and he opened the engine up, he seemed in complete control. And he nearly always won the drag races on Meadow Road.

These were impromptu contests arranged when, late at night, a car pulled up next to Cal at a stoplight and the driver gunned his engine. Then we raced from light to light until one or the other of us said, "We'll meet you at Meadow Road." The word, somehow or other, got back to the Hickory Pit and by the time Cal and his adversary got to the meeting place a crowd had gathered at what everyone knew was the finish line, a point just before the quarter mile straightaway ended in a sharp curve.

Meadow Road ran through one of the wealthiest sections of Buckhead and what I remember, as vividly as I remember the races, are the massive mansions that loomed high on the hills that rose on both sides of the road — dark shapes rising above immaculately kept lawns and spreading oaks and elms and dogwoods. We knew we didn't have very long before someone (who? who lived in those houses?) called the police — time for one, maybe two quick races before we heard the wail of the siren. (Why, I used to wonder, do they warn us? Why don't they sneak up on us? Now I realize that they wanted to warn us, wanted us to clear out before they got there. Only the very stupid or very drunk ever got caught.) When Cal won, he won going away by a large margin, but whenever he lost, the race was close. The reason seemed obvious: the sharp curve that came up just after the finish line. Cal feared the curve, feared it so much that he always eased off just before the finish line, and in close races his fear caused him to lose. I asked him about it once and he was so surprised that someone had noticed that, before he knew it, he said, "That's right. I panic. I see that curve coming up and I panic. I can't think about anything but that curve." Then he looked away, too ashamed to ask me

172

not to tell anyone else. And after that, I wasn't so afraid during our wild rides along Peachtree-Dunwoody.

But there were no sharp curves at the Fairburn drag-strip, only a concrete straightaway lying in a vast semi-urban wasteland between the city, whose skyline rose to the northeast, and the hill country of middle Georgia, the old plantation black belt. A nightmare landscape that Billy Ray entered from the south, Cal from the north. And though the races were inevitably close, Cal always lost.

So it's just as well that Miranda never came to any of those contests. Hearing about his losing was one thing, actually seeing it another. But none of the rest of us were making out any better than Cal. Even my poor father was pulled into our vortex. For he seemed to be losing as well. At least to hear my mother tell it.

"Calvin, please let me call the exterminators."

"Hell, no. I won't be cheated by those people. Anybody can get rid of rats."

"That's what you've said for years about the cockroaches."

"One ran across my face last night."

"Oh, Kate, be quiet."

"It did. Right across my face. I woke up and . . ."

"Woke up," my father said. "You claim you never sleep. How could you wake up?"

"Laugh at me. Go on. But you'll miss me when I'm dead and gone."

"Calvin, the rats are . . ."

"I'll get rid of them."

But he didn't. In desperation he took to checking his traps at night, though what he hoped to accomplish by that I don't know. But as I lay awake at night in my upstairs bedroom, fantasizing about Miranda, the rooms below me often seemed alive with activity — my father checking for rats, my grandmother checking her clock. I often wondered if they ever bumped into each other.

By day Miranda was not a fantasy but a real presence, sitting in the old concrete stands watching practice and talking to friends. All around her the trees were dying, the leaves were turning yellow, even the weeds were withering under the merciless sun. But she was as cool and as fresh as a May trout stream. Cromsky saw her too and in the locker room after practice he said, "That Miranda, she come to see me." And he winked. I stood under a cold shower and waited.

Waited week after week to be the hero. And week after week I just played. I did my job, made a few mistakes that cost us nothing, made a few good plays that gained us nothing. And then one Friday night in October the weather turned crisp and cool and the mist was like cold water on my skin and the green field shone brilliantly under the floodlight. The weather abolished the pain, suffering and drudgery in the blistering humidity of dog days. The stands were full. Somewhere in the crowd was Miranda. And my father and mother. This game would be different, somehow or other. This was the first game and I knew what the coaches had told us was true: skill and ability and brains help but what really counts is enthusiasm, "wanting it." Desire transforms a person.

And so it wasn't surprising that early in the first quarter I found myself alone, facing a fullback who lowered his head and came straight at me. I lowered my head and bulled through him. At the last moment he tried to twist away and I hit him in the middle of his spin. He went down with a scream of pain that blotted out the roar of the crowd. Still screaming, he rolled over on his back and I looked at his leg. His kneecap was not where it was supposed to be; it had slipped around to the side of his leg. His face was red and covered with sweat and his eyes, large and round and gaping like rotted orange halves, stared out at me as though he was seeing the world for the first time and was startled by it. He cried quietly as they carried him off the field.

My teammates patted me on the back. The crowd, a faceless roaring mob, urged me — all of us — on. I tried to get the fullback's knee, his face, out of my mind. I didn't know whether I was afraid or sick. I fell back into the routine that practice and the previous games had drilled into me. My mind began to click automatically.

You did what you were supposed to do. He left you no choice.

By half-time the ritual had taken over and I was telling myself that I would do it again. That you had to go full speed all the time. It could have been me. The second half was a chaos of bodies and shouts that all came to nothing on the scoreboard, for by the end of the game the score was tied. They would try a pass but a long pass was hopeless. A screen pass, I thought, and decided to gamble. At the snap of the ball I broke into their backfield and found that I had guessed right. The ball hit me squarely in the stomach and I ran the fifty yards to the goal line untouched.

We had won. In the locker room after the game I was cheered and praised and I thought of my father, how he must be with all the other fathers, proud, beaming.

That boy of yours sure showed them.

He sure as hell did.

And of course I thought of Miranda.

When I came out of the locker room after showering and dressing, she was waiting. She stood alone by the fence. Behind her the practice field lay in dark barren serenity. Cromsky saw her too and went immediately to her. They spoke for a few moments and then he went away.

When I got close to her I could smell perfume. Her sweater rode her breasts like a second skin and her words — whatever they were — meant nothing. My emotions were a riot within me, and my mind was filled with warm smooth skin. All I heard was that she would slip out and wait in the bushes beside her house. I would go home and get the family car.

I walked home, replaying the game in my mind and replaying the image of Miranda standing by the fence, the smell of her perfume, her sweater, her lips forming my name. I remembered Vicki and the arc of my curious object in the sunlight. The game, my game-saving play, the night itself were parts of a spontaneous certitude. I was coming back. Just like I said I would before Vicki drifted away, betrayed me.

The living room was dark. The smell of mildew — the smell of the long humid summer drifting up from the basement — filled my nostrils. And when I pressed the switch and the room took shape in the dim yellow light, it seemed smaller than usual. The sofa with the lace antimacassar was enormous. On the marble table were the red souvenir glasses, each inscribed with a name and date: Hallie 1904; Bessie 1912. Then I saw my father.

He was sitting in the maroon overstuffed chair, slumped slightly forward. Beside him on the floor was a bottle. The light fell across his chest. I couldn't see his face. He was breathing deeply, evenly.

Passed out, I thought. I looked up over the clock on the mantlepiece and saw the picture of my dead grandfather.

"You little son of a bitch."

My father's voice. He was drunk. Maybe he was joking.

"Were you at the game?"

"No."

"You should have been there. I . . ."

"What do I care about the game? What do I care about you or about what you did?"

I still couldn't see the face, the expression on it, but there was no humor in the voice.

"What do you mean?"

"Think I'm a failure, don't you?"

"No. I mean . . ."

"Think I'm a failure. Think I don't know what I'm doing. But you spend my money, goddam it."

"I don't know what you're talking about."

"Oh, yes, you do."

He leaned forward and his face came into the light. Not like the other time, when he stood on the porch. Now the face was twisted, the eyes bloodshot. "Well, look, goddam it." His voice was growing louder. "Look!" His hand shot forward out of the shadow. It held a rat trap and dangling from the trap, its head caught under the metal arm, was a large rat. "There, you son of a bitch. I caught the thing. And I'll catch the others, too."

I didn't know what to say. I stood there, staring at the rat, at my father's face that was partially blocked by it.

"Get out." Another voice. My mother's. She was standing in the passageway between the living room and dining room, a dark shape, a voice.

"What's wrong? What is it?"

"Just get out."

"You son of a bitch." My father rose from the chair, swayed. Then his arm shot forward and he hurled the rat at me. It missed me, of course, knocked over a lamp and slammed against the wall.

"For God's sake, get out."

But he was already on me, pressing against me. I tried to hold him off. He swung and his fist went harmlessly behind my head. I pushed him. Not hard. I was just trying to get free. But it was enough. He stumbled back, hit the chair, lost his balance and fell sprawling on the floor. I could see his eyes, his bloodshot eyes. They were accusing me of something.

My first instinct was to go to him, to help him up, to apologize. I made a move in his direction but my mother was already kneeling by his side. "Just leave," she said. "He'll be all right. Don't worry."

"But . . ."

"Go. Please go."

I stood outside in the cool air. I thought I could hear my father crying so I moved away from the house, down the steps and onto the front lawn. I saw the swatch of Spanish moss hanging from the dogwood tree. I looked up. Clouds drifted in front of the moon, blown by the same wind that was blowing my hair, cooling the sweat on my face and arms.

Miranda was waiting for me. I could still take the car. I knew how to start it without the key. But I didn't want to go. All my desire had faded into the face of my father, the voice of my mother. Yet I had to go. Not out of duty or obligation. It had taken only an instant, only the feel of my father's body beneath my hands, to abolish years of "moral" training. And I didn't act out of rebellion. I longed to go back into the house, to put my arms around him, to tell my mother that it was all right, that I under-stood. But of course I didn't understand — or rather, I didn't know what I understood. Now I know that I responded to the deepest of instincts, the overwhelming feeling that if I didn't go then, I would never go.

Miranda emerged from the bushes and slipped into the car. "Turn off the lights," she whispered and we drove off in darkness.

"What took you so long?"

"I had to hot-wire the car. My old man wouldn't let me have it."

"Won't he find out that you took it?"

"No, no, he won't find out. Where . . . where do you want to go?"

"I don't know. Let's go somewhere and talk."

I knew of one place, the acres-large parking lot behind the Baptist church. Far enough behind it so that you couldn't see it, only, if you looked hard, the steeple rising above the line of trees. Unlike other places where people went to park — driveways of empty houses, Bagley Park, North Fulton Park — I knew that no one ever drove through the church parking lot and, more important, that the police never checked it.

Even as I stopped the car and turned off the lights, I couldn't believe that anything would happen. That Miranda, who could have anyone, would have anything to do with me. Never mind that she had come. People make mistakes. Maybe she had thought that I would take her to where other people were. But no, she had suggested that we . . . go somewhere and talk. It didn't make sense. And it made even less sense when she slid across the seat and kissed me. And then sense, along with my father and mother and that terrible scene in the living room, vanished. Vanished with her clothes that fell into the back seat, onto the floor of the front seat. And then I was on her side of the seat and she was astraddle me, just above me, holding back, and I knew that no wounded brother, no irate father would appear in any doorway. I pushed her down but she resisted.

"No," she said.

"Come on."

"No. We can't."

"Why not?"

"It's not right. Something might happen."

"No. I won't let it. Just for a minute."

"No. I'll do it for you the other way."

She leaned forward a little and I could see her face clearly. It wasn't confused or panic-stricken or urgent. It had on it a look of assurance, of supreme confidence. "It's all right, honey. I'll make it all right for you." Her voice matched her face. She was in control, complete control. Her bare breasts were inches from my face, her knees were pressed against the outside of my legs. And she was in control. Maybe if I hadn't just seen my father, drunk, dangling a rat in front of him. Maybe if I hadn't just heard my mother's soft voice telling me to leave. Maybe if I hadn't seen the steeple of the church rising in the moonlight out of Miranda's naked right shoulder. Maybe then it would have been different. Maybe I wouldn't have reached up and placed my hands on top of her shoulders and thrust her violently down. And if I hadn't done that I never would have seen the look on her face change, never would have seen the confidence vanish to be replaced by . . . surprise, fear, pain, ecstasy. I couldn't tell, and then her head was next to mine, her forehead pressed against the seat. And I closed my eyes and couldn't see anything but shapes and colors pulsating in the dark.

"You shouldn't have," she said. We had coasted, lightless, to a stop beside her house.

"I thought . . . I thought you wanted to."

"You made me. You made me do it."

"No. I mean . . ." I tried, as I was to try over and over again, to reenact the scene, to read her expression. "You let me do everything else. How was I to . . ."

"*You* wanted to do all those other things. I was just trying to please you. But you didn't have any right to do what you did. Now what'll happen?"

"What do you mean?

"You know what I mean."

"But . . . but that doesn't matter. I mean, I'll . . . I won't leave you alone."

"Oh, I don't mean that. I mean, now you'll tell everybody. My reputation will be ruined."

"That's not true. I won't tell anyone."

She got out of the car, eased the door shut and then thrust her head slightly through the open window into the car. "You raped me," she said in a loud whisper. "Just remember that. You raped me."

Her words followed me back to my house. I rolled the car into the driveway and got out. But I couldn't go into the house. Not yet. I started walking and found myself a few minutes later standing by the lake. All the houses around it were dark, and the old weeping willow was a dark mass of strands falling into the water. The glow from a streetlight pulsated on the surface, came and went. I followed my eyes into the flickering movement, became lost in it, lost in the enormous silence. Everything drifted by in fragments: the twisted faces of the fullback and of my father, the stripe of the goal line passing beneath my feet; Miranda's naked body, what I felt after I pushed that body down and the look on her face, the look I couldn't read. What had I won? What had I lost? I was afraid. Afraid of what seemed to be an inevitable mixture of pleasure and pain, of success and failure. Far in the distance a dog howled.

I went back to the house, back through the dark living room to the hall, but instead of going up to my room I went down the steps into the basement. I stood for a long time, letting my eyes adjust to the darkness, and then I could make out the old blanket hanging from its nail, the bookcase with the mildewed books. "No," I whispered. "I couldn't have. I'd never do that."

No one answered. No voice from the past came to comfort me.

"She wanted me to. I wouldn't have done it if she hadn't wanted me to."

And then I saw Allen's body, Minnie's face coming out of the smoke.

"No. I couldn't have enjoyed it. I couldn't have."

The fullback's face rose from the darkness, and the eyes, large and round and gaping like rotten orange halves, accused me. And then I found that I was staring at a dead rat caught in one of my father's traps. And his eyes were the fullback's eyes, were Miranda's eyes.

"Oh, God, what have I done?" I cried aloud. But no one heard, no one came. The house drifted silently above me, drifted with the clouds and the stars.

Maybe I had raped her. Maybe I had ruined her. A sense of shame overpowered me, and all my fantasies turned into nightmares in which Miranda, because of me, became nothing more than a whore, used and abused by all my friends. I had to save her from that but every time I asked her if she would ever go out with me again, the same vacant stare went through me and the same flat voice said, "Maybe."

And still we all swirled around her, even Billy. When basketball practice started, I saw him leaning against the side of the gym on cool afternoons, dressed in only his shorts, twirling a basketball on his finger in a ludicrous attempt to impress Miranda, seated far away in the football stands, her eyes riveted on the thickly padded players. As with Cal, it remained to be seen which of his passions would finally win out.

Was anybody winning out? Try as I might, I couldn't get Miranda to go out with me again. I could hardly get her to sit next to me in Wender and Roberts drugstore. When I did, I asked again and again if she was all right, if she would forgive me, if she would go out with me. And always she looked beyond me or down into her Coke and said, "Maybe."

In December, just before Christmas, Bud died and Bessie and Mary came to arrange the funeral. They appeared dressed all in black like ghosts from those summers of years ago. Probably they looked older. I couldn't tell. Mary still smiled sweetly through her moist eyes and Bessie was still loud and a little vulgar. But mostly they seemed more than ever like the past come to bury a brother who had been living in that past since the Depression. My grandmother eyed them suspiciously, and it wasn't long before I knew why. Mary pulled me to her and I wondered how I had ever thought that she was a big woman. "Do you still work the puzzles?" she asked.

"Sometimes."

Actually, I hadn't done one in years, but it seemed like a betrayal to tell her the truth.

Her question brought back those long August afternoons and what she said at the family reunion in Piedmont Park. Now I understood a little better what she meant. Just as I understood a little better what my father had meant about Allen.

After they were gone, my grandmother said, "Good riddance."

"Why? What's wrong with them?"

She made a face. "Maybe that's what the rats were all about. Maybe they meant Bud."

Whatever they meant, they were gone. My father hadn't trapped them all. He had finally turned to poison. And when days and then weeks went by without any signs of them, we assumed they were gone. But it was a silent assumption. He never mentioned the rats again, just as he never mentioned that night. Like almost everything else between us, it was all reduced to silence.

Looking back, I realize that, considering the world I grew up in, silence was right. It was a world in which I had to ask what was natural and unnatural, a world that extolled doing, a world whose philosophy was summed up in one overwhelming cliché: "God helps those who help themselves." Not such a good philosophy when one confronts the one reality he can do nothing about. But a good philosophy if life is a game. A good philosophy for someone like Billy.

I suppose my opinion of Billy was—and is—tempered by the fact that basketball is a winter sport. Even now, thirty years later, on cold windy rainy days in January and February, I find myself in the North Fulton gym. I hear the rain beating against the metal roof, the sound echoing through the large hollow structure; how strange to be almost naked and sweating on such days. And I can smell the sweat, the oils and salves, the shorts and jerseys, the certain yet indefinable odor of sports—the gym, the locker room. And along with the smells, along with the sounds of the wind and rain, I hear the shouts of the players, piercing cries reverberating to the empty stands and back down to the court.

Billy was one of us but he was only that. One of ten, defined as much by what the others did as by what he himself did. And why were any of us even doing it, exhausting ourselves on those bitter afternoons? Because we were trying to prove ourselves. Occasionally someone, a teacher or a principal or even a coach, said we were tying to realize our full potential. But we knew better. We knew that unless our "full potential" became a reality stronger than the "full potential" of others, it was worth nothing. Else why did they keep score in games, why did they give grades in school, why was there such a thing as heaven and hell? What better metaphor for my teenage world than that gym, the warm moist womb where we prepared for the world that raged outside? But how account for the fact that some of us were stillborn, some, like myself, came out deformed and some, like Billy, came out perfect?

For Billy wasn't a natural athlete. He lacked speed and quickness and was not very well coordinated. In a crowded noisy gym on a game night you could hear the slap of his huge feet against the boards as he rumbled up and down the court. And he wasn't very tall for a center, only a little over six feet, which even thirty years ago in the all-white Atlanta high school league put him at something of a disadvantage. He was, in short, about as physically ill-equipped to be a basketball player as he was intellectually ill-equipped to be a scholar.

But Billy *wanted* to be a basketball player. He wanted it so much and worked so hard at it that he came to believe that he *deserved* to be a basketball player, that anyone who prevented him from excelling was a personal enemy. What he lacked in ability he made up for in sheer aggressiveness. Under the basket he was all elbows and knees and feet. Even his head was a dangerous weapon as he spun awkwardly on his pivot foot. He wasn't a good basketball player, but he got rebounds and he scored points.

The coach presented him to us over and over again as a model of what you can accomplish if you have *desire*. "Look at Billy," he would say. "He's slow, he's clumsy. When he first came out for the team I had trouble not laughing at him. And now he's All-City." As he spoke Billy, who was sitting with the rest of us, neither smiled nor frowned. He stared straight ahead, his eyes already filled with hatred of his next opponent, whoever he might be. I was as tall as Billy and quicker and better coordinated and I had a much better shooting eye. And yet, though we were both starters, he was the better player. I had desire; I, too, *wanted* to be a great basketball player, and when we were younger, in the eighth, ninth and tenth grades, I had been the better player. The only explanation was that I didn't have enough desire, I didn't "want it" enough. My failure was not the result of any limitation; it was my own fault, a failure of will.

Still, none of us admired Billy, mainly because we feared that our will was limited, that if we weren't born with something, we would never have it. So we attributed his success as much to stupidity and bullheadedness as to *desire*. He was simply too stupid to think that there might be some things he couldn't do, no matter how hard he tried. After all, he did badly in school, had no luck with girls, played no sport but basketball, was not funny or witty, never got drunk. But because we were so young and so poorly taught, none of us knew that the crucial quality Billy lacked wasn't intelligence. Not until my last year in high school, in the middle of a basketball game, did I come to realize the truth about Billy.

We were playing Murphy High School. They had the better team, but we were making a game of it, partly because our guards knocked the bottom out, partly because we all played defense with a vengeance, but mostly because Billy played like a whirlwind. A loud, clumsy, lumbering whirlwind but a whirlwind nonetheless. He butted, battered, banged his opponent, a somewhat bewildered beanpole who kept looking beseechingly at the referee. To no avail. So much did Billy's body go off in all directions that the poor referee probably didn't know where to start calling fouls. The beanpole retaliated by getting in the way as best he could, and the huge monster forward, the one I was guarding, began to inch in. Soon the inside game turned into a near wrestling match. My ribs, elbowed again and again, were aching; the beanpole's nose was bleeding; the monster's right eye was turning blue.

During the halftime break we slumped on the benches in the locker room. Billy was in especially bad shape: he had a cut over his left eye, he couldn't catch his breath and he rubbed his bruised thigh. But he had scored thirteen points, high for the team, high for both sides. I leaned back against a locker, barely heard Coach Russell's pep talk, and marveled over the fact that we were only

one point behind. We had done well, had played way over
our heads, but we would lose. They had more height,
more depth, more speed, more everything. I was sure
everyone else felt the same way. Not that we wouldn't
keep trying, not that we wouldn't give it everything we
had right up to the end.

The beginning of the second half seemed to bear out
what I thought. They pulled farther ahead; they were
fresher, more rested; they were, all in all, more confident,
as though they knew what I knew. Indeed, everyone
seemed to know what I knew. Our guards had slowed
down, our other forward, never a ball of fire, was merely
going through the motions, and I, though I kept moving,
was not really looking to get the ball. And even though we
were playing in their gym and Murphy was beginning to
build up the lead, the crowd was strangely quiet, as
though it was all over and they found the whole affair a
little embarrassing. It was just about at that moment that
Billy came down with a rebound, wheeled about and
faced me.

His eyes were wide open, staring, the eyes of a saint in
ecstasy or a madman in lunacy. We were about three feet
apart; had he leaned forward he would have bumped me.
I could see the beads of sweat rolling over his forehead,
down his cheeks; I could smell him, could feel his heaving
breath. It wasn't that I had never confronted him that way
before; it had happened countless times in the years we
had been playing together. But this time it was different.
This time I saw in the eyes something that had never been
there before: complete and utter oblivion, an unaware-
ness of anything save the ball in his hands and the basket
just behind him. He didn't realize that the guards had
quit, that I had quit, that even the crowd, *their* crowd,
had quit. Nobody cared anymore. Maybe that look had

been in his eyes before; maybe it had been there from the very first time he ever played; maybe the look was *why* he played. Maybe. But for the first time I saw it for what it was. Not that I *knew*, but I felt, intuited what it was. And it froze me. I stood there like a statue as he stepped forward and executed one of his ludicrous hook shots. And I watched the ball bang off rim and backboard, spin around the cylinder and fall through.

It doesn't really matter that we went on to win the game. It doesn't matter that it was probably Billy who caused us to win, who "fired us up," as we used to say in those days. What mattered was his expression, the look in his eyes.

It was that expression that rose before me as I stared into the twisted face of my grandmother a week later. And as the night stretched out toward morning other faces came out of the dark—Vicki's father's eyes and Marilyn's eyes and the bloodshot eyes of my father and Mary's moist eyes. I was back in the basement again, back with the past. Only now my grandmother was not drifting overhead; she was stretched out on the bed before me. And occasionally, when she awoke from whatever sleep held her, her good eye locked on me while the other eye stared wild and unseeing off into the darkness. The eye of her helpless right side, the side the stroke had paralyzed, struck dead. The left side struggled against death.

This her third stroke had come in the middle of the night. She had cried out and my mother had heard her. I was told this. I wasn't there. I was at a drive-in restaurant listening to Blind Willie sing bawdy songs.

> The ice man is a nice man
> Brings me ice every day
> Likes to hold me close
> And says I never have to pay.

189

I know a woman
House painted green
Got a nice box
But she won't keep it clean.

Those songs and others ran idiotically through my head as I watched my grandmother's agony. Miranda had been there, was supposed to be there with me, had promised to slip out again, to meet me by the bushes. But she hadn't been there and then she was leaning against a car, someone else's car, watching the blind man play the twelve string guitar and sing. Whose car? A souped up '39 Ford coupe. "I'd know it anywhere," Cal said. "Seen her in it lots of times."

"You lie."

"Nope. No lie. Matter of fact, I raced him about a week ago. Night after the basketball game against Murphy. You know. When Billy was the big hero. She was with him then."

And maybe that was it. Maybe all I had had to do was ask. And get there first, of course. How many others had she been waiting for?

And what was my grandmother waiting for? What did she expect? I wasn't there out of love. No, I was there out of duty. Action. *Doing*. Not that I didn't love her, but I wouldn't have been there if I hadn't had to be, if we hadn't been taking turns sitting with her in the public ward of Crawford Long hospital because obviously we couldn't afford a nurse and now it was my turn. And as the good eye locked on me so the good hand locked on my hand and the half of the mouth that worked tried to say something.

"What?"

A mumble. Then the eye closed, then the hand loosened its grip. There was a rhythm to it. I could get up for a moment, walk to the window and stare out at the bright flaring lights that illuminated the work going on several blocks away, the continuous pouring of concrete for the first Atlanta freeway — Expressway, the city fathers called it. Maybe for some reason they had to keep pouring night and day or maybe they were trying to beat a deadline.

I heard the sheets rustle and went back to my grandmother. And on it went through the night. I moved back and forth between the eye of my grandmother and the lights of the Expressway, until finally I realized that I had stood at the window longer than usual and I knew that I had felt her grip loosen for the last time, that like Miranda she hadn't waited for me. But once again I couldn't tell if I had won or lost.

My grandmother's crossed hands were winter fields — pale, bony, streaked here and there with black, and utterly still. The same winter fields were there in the face but the undertaker had covered them with paint, had pulled the frozen ruts out smooth with wax, and had closed the hard cold suns to suggest sleep rather than death.

The room was filled with relatives. Uncle Thad, his stomach still falling over his belt, and Aunt Molly. Uncle Walter, large and prosperous. My father, composed, even a little cheerful in unguarded moments. Mr. and Mrs. Simpkins. And a whirl of faces and bodies from middle Georgia: relatives I dimly remembered from other funerals, from family reunions in Piedmont Park. One after another they spoke to my mother and time after time she told them how she didn't regret all that she had had to do.

"It's all so lovely," she said. "Everyone has been so nice, so thoughtful."

Uncle Walter slipped his arm around her shoulders. "They all know how wonderful you were, Sister. You treated her like she was your own mother."

She looked up at her brother and smiled.

And Aunt Mary. She had come back. Only a month before she had ridden the bus from Charlotte through the cold winter air and now she had ridden it again. I imagined her sitting in the bus, staring at the sun hanging low on the horizon, perfectly round and the color of the ice that seemed to radiate from it out over the land. Grandmother had hoped that it was she and Bessie that the rats had brought, that the rats had signaled Bud's death. But she knew better, really. The suspicious look in her eye should have told me that she knew better.

Mary hovered as always on the periphery of things, a black shape speaking quietly to people who seemed to have no one else to speak to. I was thinking about her, remembering those summers before she stopped coming, when I heard someone shout.

"Margaret!"

I turned and saw in the doorway a gray-headed man with a red face. He was wearing an old double-breasted blue suit, now at least two sizes too large for him. The knot of his tie was stuffed under one of the curling collars of a dingy white shirt. His shoes were paint-spattered brogans bulging out from beneath the wrinkled folds and cuffs of his trousers.

Uncle Luther had come to the funeral. ("No need to tell him about it; no telling what he would do if he came," Uncle Walter had said.)

"Margaret!" he shouted again to his sister and over-powered the room with the unmistakable odor of Four

Roses. Tears filled his eyes which had turned to the casket. "Kate!" He half stumbled toward the dead woman.
Before anyone realized what was happening he was leaning over the corpse, kissing the painted face. Walter was
rushing toward him when Luther ran his hand over her
head and knocked off the wig, revealing the straggly hair
beneath, and for an instant my grandmother's real face,
fierce and implacable, broke through the rouge and wax,
as though she were accusing Luther one last time before
they lowered her into the frozen ground. Walter pulled
him away and two aunts were immediately at the casket,
repairing the damage. He threw his arms around his
sister and sobbed uncontrollably until she started sobbing
as well.

"All right, all right," my father said, and he and Walter
pulled him away. Luther looked at each in turn and then
at me. They got him more or less calmed down, and the
others, sympathizing with the plight of the family since
they all had their drunken brothers as well, began to slip
out of the room to the chapel.

"He'll have to sit with the family," Walter said in
exasperation and my father nodded. After a brief alterca-
tion, during which Luther insisted upon being a pall-
bearer and Walter insisted that the pallbearers had
already been chosen, and anyway, he was a member of
the "immediate family," they led him into the small area
to the side of the coffin reserved for the family. He
sobbed loudly through the ceremony.

He got into the funeral home limousine with my
mother and father, Uncle Walter (his wife was too ill to
attend), my sister (my brother didn't come home for the
funeral) and myself for the ride to the cemetery. The
hearse, followed by the long line of cars, crawled through
the grim winter streets of the city, holding up frustrated

drivers at busy intersections. In the limousine Luther talked. And sang.

"I'm glad they sang 'In the Garden.' It's my favorite. It was beautiful. The preacher, he said just the right things. And then they sang 'In the Garden.'"

Silence.

"She was a wonderful old woman. Wonderful. You were a lucky man to be raised by her, Calvin. A lucky man."

Silence.

Then, in a quivering, off-key voice interrupted as he went along by jerky sobs:

> *I come to the garden alone,*
> *While the dew is still on the roses.*

"Luther, for God's sake," said Walter.

"That's the one. That's the one." He thrust his face forward so that it was only an inch or so from my mother's. "I want that sung when my time comes," he said.

"Luther, be quiet," Uncle Walter hissed.

"I mean it. It's the only song I want sung." He settled back, leaned his head against the window, and began again.

> *And He walks with me, and He talks with me,*
> *And He tells me I am His own;*
> *And the joy we share as we tarry there,*
> *None other has ever known.*

I tried to escape by concentrating on the districts we were passing through, mostly warehouse and manufacturing areas, gray and somber in the cold February air, but it was not a part of the city I knew. It was only a place you passed through going south, leaving the city, but not a place you ever went to if you lived on the northside, in Buckhead. I remembered those times I had driven through it on the way to see Minnie years ago, the barren deserted farmland, the old rotting shacks, the rusting hulks of cars. And I remembered driving through it on that rainy night on the way to Uncle Thad's house. It hadn't changed much. The city had gone in the other direction, had left this part of the world for the failures.

Luther sang and cried all the way to the cemetery, at the end the song indistinguishable from the crying, from his wailful plea that "In the Garden" be the only song sung when "my time comes."

At graveside, as the icy wind caused the canvas awning over the grave to flap loudly, I watched him closely and wondered how he could stand the cold without a coat, even as drunk as he was. But he continued to sing from time to time, much to the distress of the preacher who had trouble making himself heard above the noise of the flapping canvas and the drunken brother of the daughter-in-law of the deceased. Finally Walter hissed in my ear, "For God's sake get him out of here for awhile," and I led him off among the nearby tombstones while a small group of relatives and friends stood by the grave talking. Luther lapsed into silence, asked for a cigarette, started singing again, then stopped and peered at me. He leaned forward and I realized that he was trying to figure out who I was. "Why, you're Margaret's boy, aren't you?"

I nodded.

He leaned further forward to shake my hand and lost his balance. I reached out and caught him. The body beneath my hands was a mass of shivering bones and it occurred to me that the weather could easily kill him.

"Oooops!" he said and straightened up, bracing him-self against a tombstone. "You ever been to the Fox Theater?"

"Yes."

"I did all the ornamental plastering in it. I was mak-ing a hundred dollars a week during the depression. A hundred dollars. While everybody else was in breadlines. Did you know that?"

"And then the army drafted you. I know."

"Drafted me? Hell, no, I joined. I had to beg 'em to take me. Had a heart murmur, you know." He waved his arm in the direction of the people gathered around the grave, slipped, half-fell and caught himself. "The army. The war. That's all they ever talk to me about. But not her, not the old girl."

"You mean my grandmother."

"That's her. That's the old girl. God, she was a feisty one, wasn't she?"

I stared at him and said nothing.

"Lemme tell you something, boy." He reached out for the lapel of my coat, miraculously found it and pulled me up against him. "Even when I was earning a hundred dollars a week, Mimi wouldn't speak to me when I had my work clothes on. You know that? She'd pass me on the street and I'd say, 'Hi, Mimi,' and her in that fancy hat I'd just bought her, she'd just walk by and wouldn't speak. Whoooeee! What a woman. God almighty! Lemme tell you something, boy, you split that woman's head down the middle, you'd find hats on one side and shoes on the other."

He broke into a wild fit of laughter which turned his face blood red and caused his eyes to bulge. I reached out to hold him but he pushed me away and fell back against the tombstone. "She left me, left me. Walked out 'cause I

196

traveled too much." He burst into tears. "Now how the hell do you figure that? Wouldn't speak to me on the street, then left me 'cause I traveled too much." He ran his hand over his nose and sniffed loudly.

"Come on, Uncle Luther, you better . . ."

"On September 21, 1941, she just said, 'I'm leaving you, Luther,' and she walked out and I never saw her again." He fell silent and I wondered if, in his drunken haze, he was reliving the day, the hour, the instant. But then I heard the plaintive whine.

> *O I come to the garden alone,*
> *While the dew is still on the roses.*

I couldn't stand it anymore. Him. His lunatic singing. His drunken sentimentality. I reached out, grabbed his bony shoulders and shook him.

"Why the hell did you come to the funeral? Why?!"

For the first time I felt that I had made some kind of contact with him. He stopped singing, looked at me in surprise and said, "To pay my last respects to the old girl. She knew, dammit, she knew!"

I heard someone call my name. I turned. My father was motioning to me. I looked back at Luther. He was staring at the ground, singing once again.

"Come on," I said, "we have to go back."

I caught him by the elbow and led him back to the grave. He stumbled along, half singing, half recalling his depression days. When he was close enough, he shouted, "Margaret!" and pulled away from me and fell into his sister's arms.

Walter agreed to take him to the station and put him on a bus to Gainesville and as he pulled him down the hill to the car, Luther looked back over his shoulder and cried, "I just wanted to pay my last respects!"

I looked at the two men standing next to each other: one in a trim, dark blue, tailored suit with a rather jaunty hat and shoes that shined brightly; the other in trousers the crotch of which sagged almost to his knees and cuffs that swallowed his brogans. And suddenly I felt profoundly sorry for Luther, so sorry that I intervened and led him around the car to help him in from the other side so that I could say to him, "It wasn't your fault. None of it was."

His head snapped up and his eyes were suddenly clear with anger. It was as though he had stepped off-stage and pulled off his own wig. "Then who the hell's fault was it," he snarled. "Christ, you're just like the rest of them."

After the car had pulled away, my father asked, "What in the world were you talking about all that time?"

"Oh, I don't know. He didn't make much sense."

"The war, I'll bet. That's all he ever talked about. The damn war."

"It ruined him," my mother said. "No wonder he kept looking back to it. It ruined him."

My father and mother and sister went home with a cousin; I stayed behind to gather up some of the flowers to take back to the house. I went up and down the hill several times, hauling irises, hydrangeas, gardenias, roses to the trunk and back seat. Tired and cold, I stood by the grave for a moment before taking the last load to the car. The mound rose gently above the surrounding ground and was covered by a thick green mat.

I think that I expected an omen, some sign or revelation that would make it all fall into a pattern. I looked up from the grave to the surrounding cemetery that stretched as far as I could see in all directions except one, where a main road a quarter of a mile away hummed with traffic. In the other directions were the low rolling tombstone-covered hills, the massive squat mausoleum, a high concrete pillar commemorating the Confederate dead, and the huge naked shade trees, gray against the gray sky. Finally I picked up the vase I had come back for, a vase filled with roses.

-3-

When we played Murphy a second time, they beat us (the fight at the end of that game was much better than the game itself); and when we played them for the city championship, they beat us again. And we ended the season by losing in the first round of the state tournament. By then it was early March, and the wind outside the gym no longer howled but whispered of spring; the rain fell softly on the roof, and when we came out it was still light and there were birds singing in the trees.

And when in the spring it was announced that the dragstrip would shut down to make way for an "industrial park," Cal grew desperate. He disappeared for longer periods than usual, refused to talk to us at all when we came by to visit. It was our senior year and we were all afflicted with the sense of an ending, but it hardly seemed to matter to Cal that our high school days were coming to an end, that soon we would go our separate ways; all that mattered to him was Billy Ray.

The last race took place on May 1, and several of us accompanied him to the dragstrip. His race was scheduled last and Billy Ray fiddled with his car right up to starting time, but Cal merely leaned against his front fender and never even raised the hood. "It's set," he said over and over again. "I've finally got it figured out." What "it" was none of us knew, and long ago Cal had given up trying to explain the mysteries of the internal combustion engine.

Did Billy Ray look especially grubby that day? Was his hair especially greasy, his T-shirt especially torn and dirty? Cal, on the other hand, had on spotless mechanic's overalls and looked for all the world like an engineer in an experimental laboratory. He knew—and I suspect Billy

Ray knew—that this was not only the last race; it was the only race. None of the others mattered. Whoever won today would be the winner for all time.

We—all Cal's friends—were bunched along the finish line, but as the starter held the flag aloft, I could imagine Cal's face because it hadn't changed for a month—bland and expressionless, as though the slightest sign of emotion might take something away from his firm resolve. There was a moment of silence during which we stared over at the two rednecks—one male, the other female—who had come with Billy Ray. They stared back at us, at our clean loafers and clean blue jeans and trim crew cuts, and maybe I only imagined a glint of hatred in their eyes. And then the flag fell.

It was close all the way, from the deafening squeal of tires at the start to the roar as the cars flew by us. Too close to call, a dead heat surely, but after a brief conference the judges declared Billy Ray the winner.

We were outraged. The judges—obviously rednecks themselves, maybe even related to Billy Ray—had cheated Cal. We screamed, we booed. Several of us charged the judges and argued with them. All to no avail. Looking back, I realize that there was only one trophy and they had to award it to someone. Who knows? Maybe they flipped a coin.

In our fury we forgot about Cal, who, as we were screaming and arguing and stomping about, had wandered off to the edge of the dragstrip and onto the red clay and weeds that stretched over acres to the distant highway. I went to him, came up behind him and put my hand on his shoulder. "You got screwed," I said. "We all saw it. It was a tie."

He didn't say anything. He didn't even turn his head. "They're all rednecks," I said.

"It doesn't matter," he mumbled.

"Of course it doesn't. You know you . . ."

"No, I mean it doesn't matter that they're rednecks. Or that they cheated me. None of that matters." He turned his head and I saw that he was crying. Tears streamed down his face. "I didn't beat him. A tie doesn't mean anything. I didn't beat him. I couldn't ever beat him. Not in a million years."

But it wasn't long before he was the old Cal again, shuffling along with his duck-footed walk, partying with the rest of us during that last month of school. There was one important change: he now drove his own car all the time. We didn't think much of that. After all, what was there to save it for? And he certainly didn't save it. He spun the wheels at every light, jammed and popped the gears, slammed the door unmercifully. He was, we thought, putting Billy Ray and a year of failure behind him just as the rest of us were putting high school behind us during that frantic month.

We were receiving news from the colleges we had applied to, acceptances from Davidson and Vanderbilt and Duke. But not Billy. He applied and was accepted, along with everyone who couldn't get in anywhere else, at the state university. Only recently, at the class reunion, did I find out what happened. He entertained us by telling how the counselor, having looked over his grades and his IQ test scores and his college boards, advised him not to go to college. And we all laughed at the stupidity of someone telling a famous surgeon that he shouldn't go to college. Looking back, I can imagine the scene: the kindly old woman telling him he will be much happier if he goes in for vocational training; Billy staring at her with those uncomprehending eyes. She was right, of course. But probably he was already shifting from basketball to medicine, already deciding — as illogically as he had decided to play basketball when he was nine or ten — to become a doctor.

Classwork was finished and we spent the evenings roaming Buckhead, refusing to admit that it was boring, that the fun had gone out of it. One night I was riding with Cal when a car ahead of us began to slow down and weave from one side of the road to the other. At first we thought the driver was trying to block us — an old game — but soon we realized that he was drunk, and for some reason — probably idle curiosity that grew from boredom and aimless rambling — we followed the car. It turned on Lenox Road and then turned again and we found ourselves on a dirt road leading into Johnsontown. The car ahead stopped and we stopped and shut off the headlights.

We were suddenly plunged into darkness. I smelled coal and wood smoke and heard the yapping of dogs, and as my eyes adjusted to moonlight I saw the ramshackle houses that lined either side of the road, made out the scrawny pines and red clay yards. We had crossed a border, driven into a foreign land. Not that I hadn't been in black neighborhoods before, but they had always been far away — south Atlanta where the maid lived and where Westview Cemetery was; the other side of the tracks in small towns where distant relatives lived, towns slung along lonely highways. Then I had seen what I had expected to see and so I felt what I was expected to feel — pity for people who lived in such poverty. But now I was overwhelmed not by pity but by the sense of something alien — not hostile or dangerous but simply different. Only when the door of the car we were following opened and the drunk got out did I begin to be afraid. I couldn't see his eyes; he was only a dark shape. But I was sure he could see me. Somewhere a door slammed and then, in the distance, a shout, followed by something that might have been laughter, a sound that faded into faint sounds—a rustling of leaves, a murmur of voices, a song. Everything—the car, Cal, our own neighborhoods, orderly and quiet—seemed to dissolve into those sounds, those smells, and I felt for an instant that the only way out was with the smoke that I could see now, trailing up into the sky.

And then Cal was frantically turning the car around and we roared toward Lenox Road, throwing gravel and dirt into the air. I looked out the back window at the dark shape that was still leaning against the car.

I tried to piece together the boys I had played football against on those hot August days and the place they disappeared into. In the light of day as I drove down Lenox Road it was as though I was walking down a corridor so narrow I could touch both walls at the same time: the solid middle-class white suburbs and dark pungent Johnsontown. An unnatural division, surely, but no more unnatural than the city itself; indeed, it was an extension of the city, a dividing up of human beings according to the whims of human nature.

Or so it seems. I can't say for sure because all I have left are images: a dark shape on a dark night leaning against a car surrounded by shacks and smoke swirling into the sky. And the anxious face of Cal, who got me out of that dark world. Just as soon he was to get me out of a much darker one.

Not far from my house a large tract of treeless land that stood between East Wesley and Lindberg Road was being bulldozed for a housing development. From the

East Wesley side the land fell sharply into a deep narrow gully, then rose on the other side to Lindberg. The bull-dozers had pushed earth into the gully to provide a narrow passageway over it. On weekends and after working hours Cal took us there for wild joyrides. The car swayed and bumped down the steep incline, shot over the passageway and roared up the other side until he spun it around in circles. The place became known as "the ditch." "Let's go to the ditch," we'd shout and pile into Cal's car.

Several days of rain kept us from going there, and on a Saturday morning the sky was still overcast, the color of old lead. But it had stopped raining. We got into the car, three in the backseat, myself and Cal in the front, and drove to the top of the hill. Cal stopped the car.

"It's all mud," Tom said.

And it was—a quagmire dropping into the deep ditch.

"Oh, what the hell. Let's go to the Hickory Pit."

"There won't be anybody there. Let's drive out to the lake."

"And do what? There's nothing . . ."

Then we realized that the car was moving.

"Hey, we can't make it. We'll get stuck."

Cal pressed the accelerator to the floorboard; the tires dug down and pushed the car forward. Once the car was moving, the mud provided enough resistance to propel us faster and faster down the hill. The ditch rose before us, came closer and closer, but Cal didn't ease up, not even when the car careened out of the old tire ruts and began to angle away from the passageway.

I looked at Cal. His eyes were fixed dead ahead, his face expressionless. A few seconds passed, but they seemed an eternity as we hurtled toward the ditch, which rose to meet us. And suddenly Cal was fighting the steering wheel and fanning the brake pedal, urging the car to the right. I remembered Meadow Road, the curve, Cal's panic. Now his face was screwed up in something akin to pain and I even noticed the sweat pouring down his cheeks. He downshifted, turned the wheel, straightened out, turned the wheel, straightened out, got the tires to bite into the mud and the car inched to the right. But the ditch was rising faster than the car was moving to the right. We would never make it. I pushed my feet against the floorboard, braced myself, tried to say, "You can do it, Cal," but no words came out. Then Cal jerked the steering wheel as fast and as hard as he could to the right and the car began to spin. It turned once, twice. The dark sky wheeled around me until Cal threw the wheel violently back to the left and we shot sideways across the passageway and came to an abrupt halt on the other side of the ditch, mired deep in mud.

"You son of a bitch!" Tom roared from the back seat. "You almost killed us."

Cal pressed his face against the steering wheel. His whole body was trembling. Bobby reached from the back seat and grasped his shoulders. "It's all right," he whispered. "You did it. You got us over."

And in that instant I knew that that was precisely what he had done: he had gotten *us*, not himself, over.

After that spring they both disappeared. Or maybe I disappeared. I don't know the details of Cal's descent into drugs. And I don't know the details of Billy's rise from a third-rate cow college to one of the most famous medical centers in the country. But I can well imagine how he dumbfounded everyone along the way, all those poor souls who—like the beanpole who played for Murphy—could make no sense out of the academic equivalent of whirling elbows and knees and a battering ram head, who never realized until he was long out of their classes that what Billy lacked wasn't intelligence. No, what he lacked was . . . imagination.

For that's what I'd seen in his eyes that night thirty years before although I couldn't say, couldn't articulate it: an utter lack of imagination, a total inability to conceive of failure. I think that's why, over the years, that one image of Billy remained buried deep within me to rise up that night in the restaurant. There in the warm womb of the gym Billy had already decided what he would see and what he wouldn't see, and that decision is the source of all other decisions — what "masks" we'll wear, what "roles" we'll play. Why he made his decision I can't say; maybe it was forced upon him; maybe something in his life strengthened his instinct for self-preservation, made him think he could survive only by blotting out anything that threatened him. He couldn't fear what he didn't know existed, so even thirty years ago he couldn't see anything beyond the ball in his hands, the basket over his shoulder, couldn't see anything that wasn't there. But how could I, thirty years ago, know the significance of that look in his eyes, how could I know that it meant that eventually he would stand in a miserable village in Africa or Central America, would stare out at the squalor and pain and despair, and not "see anything that would be worth my son's life"?

By which, of course, he meant that he could see nothing worth his own life.

Ever since that class reunion I've been troubled by an image, sharp and clear. We — the basketball team — are leaving the gym after a practice. It's a winter evening and as we come out of the warmth of the gym, the cold wind stings my face. One of us spins a ball on his finger;

another pivots, pretends he's on the court with a ball in his hands and executes a jump shot. The rest of us crouch down in our jackets. And bringing up the rear comes Billy. Straight and stiff, he seems not to notice the cold or the spinning ball or the shouts of his teammates or the fake jump shot. Then, one by one we peel off into the dark until Billy is alone, striding along the streets I used to know so well, the streets that eventually would lead us beyond Buckhead, beyond the city. I can see his eyes. They haven't changed. He doesn't care that we've gone. Maybe he doesn't even know we've gone. After all, outside the gym he doesn't need us anymore.

The morning after the reunion I left my mother's house — my son in the den watching television, my mother in the kitchen talking to my sister — and I walked the half mile or so to a spot on Lindberg that overlooks the place where we survived that wild downhill ride.

At least I guess it was the place. The housing development had long since been completed, and what stretched beneath me was a solid middle-class neighborhood complete with lawns and shade trees. Try as I might, I couldn't figure out exactly where the ditch had been or where, on the hill facing, we began our descent. All was orderly, still and serene. Who would ever have believed that somewhere down there five boys almost died? And it occurred to me that I probably wouldn't be able to figure out where the Fairburn dragstrip had been either. Or exactly where, in the midst of Lenox Square, our makeshift football field was.

I stood there a long time but I couldn't make the houses go away, couldn't see the car spinning in the mud. What I could see, could remember, was Cal's dumpy body, his duck walk. I could hear his Yankee accent. And I heard

Miss Lee saying to him, "The correct answer is not nearly as important as the method you use to achieve it." And then I remembered Cal. And I remembered how he got me to the other side.

EPILOGUE

For me and my friends, the section of the Expressway between Peachtree and Piedmont Roads that was under construction the night my grandmother died was a place where we could drink the six-packs of beer we managed to get our hands on. A great swath of red clay dotted with earth moving machines that under moonlight looked like the hulks of prehistoric monsters. There, free from competition over grades and sports and girls, we got high and sang and told jokes and bragged about our exploits and raged against our teachers and parents.

One night I climbed to the top of one of the earth movers. In one direction I could see the red light atop the Fulton Bank building, Atlanta's first "skyscraper"; in the other direction the moon cast a pale glow over the rolling hills of north Georgia. And below me I heard the shouts and laughter of my friends. Nothing, it seemed, could violate my vision of reality: the city, the country, and between, the solid neighborhoods of Buckhead.

And then one of the others—Tom, I think—was pushing me aside. I climbed down and looked up. A little drunk, he began to fool with levers and pedals, pretending that he was operating the machine. Suddenly one of the levers he was fooling with shot forward and the huge monster began to move down the incline, slowly at first but gathering speed as it went. Tom tried to stop it, gave up, scrambled down the side and off just before it crashed into a bulldozer. Probably very little damage was done but the collision was noisy and, convinced that the police would arrive at any moment, we ran, stumbling and falling and cursing, to the car.

I don't know whether or not the police came, but the next day in the afternoon paper we read about the "act of vandalism" that had caused "extensive damage to road-building equipment." That didn't bother us; what bothered us was that we had lost one of the few safe places where we could go to drink.

I imagine that somewhere or other, surely in the newspaper graveyard and maybe in the city or county or state archives, there is an official record of the event. But since that record tells only what happened, it is irrelevant. What mattered was the expression on Tom's face when the lever shot forward and the machine began to move, his desperate effort to reverse what he had done, followed by his frantic scramble down. And how suddenly he, and all the rest of us, were cold sober.

I remember that night and then I sometimes dream that I'm in Hawley's backroom, playing the pinball machine. I see my reflection in the glass and through that image of myself lights flash and the ball richochets off the rubber bumpers. And for several minutes after I've waked up, I can hear bells ringing, smell oranges and potatoes. And I know that the old Slaton mansion, though it was torn down years ago, is still out there, waiting for me.